"It's funny," Simon said, "watching Francie come into this world, being the first person to hold her, I feel connected to her in some way."

Whenever Risa thought about Simon delivering, then handing her her baby, tears came to her eyes. It was a moment she'd never forget. It sounded as if it were a moment *he* wouldn't forget, either.

The current zipping between them almost took her breath away. The intense look in his eyes practically stopped her heart. She was so aware of the maleness of him, a sensual pull toward him that she'd never felt with any man. Simon was so virile, so strong, so…everything male. And a few months ago, that would have made her run in the other direction. But getting to know him this past week has lowered her defenses, watching him with her daughter just now had lowered them even further.

When Simon bent his head, Risa knew what was going to happen. She could have shifted away. She could have turned her head. But she didn't. She wanted to face whatever this electricity was with Simon and then deal with it.…

Dear Reader,

From a Texas sweetheart to a Chicago advice columnist, our heroines will sweep you along on their journeys to happily ever after. Don't miss the tender excitement of Silhouette Romance's modern-day fairy tales!

In *Carolina's Gone A' Courting* (SR #1734), Carolina Brubaker is on a crash course with destiny—and the man of her dreams—*if* she can survive their summer of forced togetherness! Will she lasso the heart of her ambitious rancher? Find out in the next story in Carolyn Zane's THE BRUBAKER BRIDES miniseries.

To this once-burned plain Jane a worldly, sophisticated, handsome lawyer is *not* the kind of man she wants...but her heart has other plans. Be there for the transformation of this no-nonsense woman into the beauty she was meant to be, in *My Fair Maggy* (SR #1735) by Sharon De Vita.

Catch the next installment of Cathie Linz's miniseries MEN OF HONOR, *The Marine Meets His Match* (SR #1736). His favorite independent lady has agreed to play fiancée for this military man who can't resist telling her what to do. If only he could order her to *really* fall in love....

Karen Rose Smith brings us another emotional tale of love and family with *Once Upon a Baby...* (SR #1737). This love-leery sheriff knows he should stay far away from his pretty and pregnant neighbor—he's not the husband and father type. But delivering her baby changes everything....

I hope you enjoy every page of this month's heartwarming lineup!

Mavis C. Allen
Associate Senior Editor

Please address questions and book requests to:
Silhouette Reader Service
U.S.: 3010 Walden Ave., P.O. Box 1325, Buffalo, NY 14269
Canadian: P.O. Box 609, Fort Erie, Ont. L2A 5X3

Once Upon a Baby
KAREN ROSE SMITH

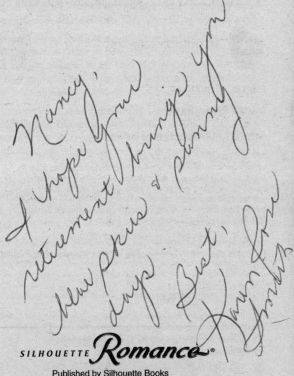

Nancy,
I hope your
retirement brings you
new places & plenty
of joys. Best,
Karen Rose
Smith

SILHOUETTE *Romance*®
Published by Silhouette Books
America's Publisher of Contemporary Romance

To Ken—May your life in Oklahoma bring you
happiness, success and fulfillment of your dreams.
Wherever you go, you're only a heart-thought away.
Love, Mom.

With thanks to Linda Goodnight, my Oklahoma contact.

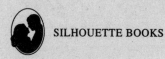 SILHOUETTE BOOKS

ISBN 0-373-19737-3

ONCE UPON A BABY...

Copyright © 2004 by Karen Rose Smith

Visit Silhouette Books at www.eHarlequin.com

Printed in U.S.A.

Books by Karen Rose Smith

Silhouette Romance

*Adam's Vow #1075
*Always Daddy #1102
*Shane's Bride #1128
†Cowboy at the Wedding #1171
†Most Eligible Dad #1174
†A Groom and a Promise #1181
The Dad Who Saved
  Christmas #1267
‡Wealth, Power and a
  Proper Wife #1320
‡ Love, Honor and a
  Pregnant Bride #1326
‡Promises, Pumpkins and
  Prince Charming #1332
The Night Before Baby #1348

‡Wishes, Waltzes and a Storybook
  Wedding #1407
Just the Man She Needed #1434
Just the Husband She Chose #1455
Her Honor-Bound Lawman #1480
Be My Bride? #1492
Tall, Dark & True #1506
Her Tycoon Boss #1523
Doctor in Demand #1536
A Husband in Her Eyes #1577
The Marriage Clause #1591
Searching for Her Prince #1612
With One Touch #1638
The Most Eligible Doctor #1692
Once Upon a Baby #1737

Silhouette Special Edition

Abigail and Mistletoe #930
The Sheriff's Proposal #1074
His Little Girl's Laughter #1426
Expecting the CEO's Baby #1535
Their Baby Bond #1588
Take a Chance on Me #1599

Silhouette Books

The Fortunes of Texas
Marry in Haste...

Montana Mavericks:
  Wedding in Whitehorn
It Happened One Wedding Night

*Darling Daddies
†The Best Men
‡Do You Take This Stranger?

Previously published under the pseudonym Kari Sutherland

Silhouette Romance

Heartfire, Homefire #973

Silhouette Special Edition

Wish on the Moon #741

KAREN ROSE SMITH

loves to write. She began putting pen to paper in high school when she discovered poetry as a creative outlet, but never suspected crafting emotional and romantic stories would become her life's work! Married for thirty-three years, she and her husband reside in Pennsylvania with their two cats, Ebbie and London. Readers can e-mail Karen through her Web site at www.karenrosesmith.com or write to her at P.O. Box 1545, Hanover, PA 17331.

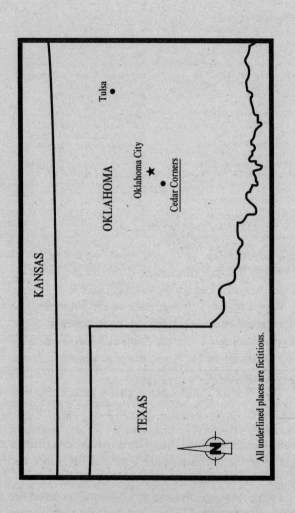

All underlined places are fictitious.

Chapter One

As Sheriff Simon Blackstone strode up the path to his house, his gaze inexorably swerved next door.

Risa Parker had just stepped outside, a watering can in her hand. At almost nine months pregnant, or there-abouts according to *his* calculations, she moved a bit slowly toward the hanging baskets of white geraniums on the front porch.

When she lifted the watering can to the hanging basket—

She doubled over!

Pushing his Stetson high on his forehead, Simon rushed across the lawn in one leap and was beside her in a few heartbeats.

"What's wrong?" he asked as his arms encircled her to provide support. She was dressed in a pink jumper today and was as beautiful as ever.

Just coming off duty, he was looking forward to a cold beer. July in Oklahoma could be smothering. But now that beer was forgotten as Risa blurted out, "Cramping. I don't know if it's the baby. It's too early." Her voice trembled, and he could feel her fear.

When he swept her up into his arms, she gasped, but not in pain this time. Her dark brown eyes were huge. "What are you doing?"

"Taking you to the hospital. With the flashing lights on my SUV, we'll get there as quick as any ambulance."

"Sheriff Blackstone..."

They'd introduced themselves way back in February when she'd thanked him for shoveling snow from her sister Janetta's walk. He'd noticed Risa as soon as she'd moved in with Janetta Lombardi at the start of the new year. Her long, wavy, chestnut hair and her classically beautiful face had kicked his libido where it was most sensitive. He'd told himself then that she was grieving over her husband's death and that she was off limits. A few months later when he'd noticed her pregnancy developing, he'd tried to erase erotic thoughts he'd had about her. He knew better than to get involved with any woman who might want commitment—and a mother-to-be certainly would. Since last February, they'd politely exchanged views on the weather. Now polite just didn't seem to be the way to go.

"It's Simon." He descended the steps with her in his arms.

"Simon, I have to lock the house, grab the bag I packed for the hospital, and—" Another contraction started. She bent forward in his arms and bit her lip.

"I'll come back for your bag if I have to. Right now, I'm getting you to a doctor."

He held onto her as the contraction ebbed away. He could see the intensity lessen as the expression on her face told him she was becoming relaxed again, at least as relaxed as she could be under the circumstances.

"All right," she agreed, her arms tightening reluctantly around his neck. There was wariness in her eyes.

That was reasonable since they were strangers.

In case she didn't like the idea of him wandering around in her sister's house, he reassured her, "I've taken an oath to uphold the law. Believe me. You can trust me."

Her gaze was steady on his for a few moments as she weighed his words. "The grapevine in Cedar Corners says you're a tough-but-fair sheriff."

"Do you believe the grapevine?"

"I have no choice at the moment."

She was right about that, and he could see she didn't like choices being taken from her hands.

Hurrying with her to the white SUV, he set her down. "I'll help you into the front seat. I don't want to put you in the back with that barrier between us." The chain-link partition had never been necessary during his term as sheriff in Cedar Corners, but a lawman never knew when he might need it.

Risa brushed her silky, thick hair behind her ear. "I'll be fine."

As Simon gazed into her dark brown eyes again, he felt a stirring that wasn't appropriate right now. "I have a feeling you say that a lot, and it isn't always true."

When her cheeks pinkened and she didn't deny his observation, he opened the front passenger-side door and lifted her inside.

The drive to Cedar Corners Community Hospital only took about seven minutes. During that time, Risa stared straight ahead and kept her hands folded over her belly. Simon told himself his pulse was racing because of the adrenaline rush of getting her to the hospital.

"How are you doing?" he asked as he pulled up in front of the emergency room.

"I'm f..." She stopped, then gave him a small smile. They both realized what she'd been about to say. "No more contractions," she added. "Maybe this isn't the real thing after all."

"And maybe it is."

The hospital's emergency room was having a slow evening, and Risa was able to get registered right away. Simon offered to find a wheelchair, but she refused.

When the technician called her back to the examining cubicles, Simon informed her, "I'll wait here. Send me word on how you're doing."

She looked surprised that he'd stay. "I don't want you to waste your time waiting."

"I'm not leaving you stranded here alone. Is there anyone I can call for you?"

At his question she looked troubled. "My sister Janetta's out of town for a few weeks. And my mom and older sister are both high-strung. They have a tendency to make mountains out of molehills and just want to take over."

Her voice was filled with exasperation, but Simon

could see she was fond of her family. That was something he knew nothing about. Whenever he thought of his mother and father, the wounds went so deep he blanked them out.

"See what your doctor says," he advised her. "If she admits you, then I'll call them for you and leave."

When Risa started to protest, he gave her an ultimatum. "It's me or your mother and sister."

She thought about it for a moment. "I'll let you know what's happening as soon as I see the doctor." Then shyly, she touched his arm. "Thank you for bringing me here."

The light, butterflylike feel of her fingers on his forearm sent Simon's adrenaline rushing through him full blast again. Seconds later, Risa was following the technician through the door into the emergency room beyond.

After she'd gone, Simon could still feel the imprint of her small feminine fingers on his skin. He swore silently because just that brief touch had aroused him more than he dared to admit.

A half hour later, Risa was walking the halls of the emergency room as her doctor had suggested. She still felt shaken by the events of the last hour or so and not only because of the contractions. The past year of her life had brought more upheaval than the twenty-five years that had gone before it. After she'd graduated from college, she'd taught elementary school while earning her master's as a reading specialist. She'd been working with children with reading problems for a year when she'd met the charming Dr. Todd Parker and married him. After they were married, Todd had turned out to be less than charming.

Out of the blue he'd wanted her to quit her job, join the garden club, lunch with other doctors' wives and help promote his bid for chief of staff of the hospital. Raised by a mother who practically waited on her dad hand and foot, Risa had considered it her duty to support Todd's ambitions. Yet his demand for her to quit her job had turned into other demands, and his wishes had become the only ones that mattered. He'd found ways of belittling her and had insidiously eroded her self-confidence. After a year of society matrons' meetings, serving on charitable boards and generally being a trophy wife, she'd realized she needed to go back to working with children to give her life meaning. Todd had been adamantly opposed, but she'd stood her ground. His silence, curt replies and disapproval had lasted for weeks, and their marriage had disintegrated day by day as she realized over the two years they'd been married, she'd become someone she didn't want to be.

Then that awful night...

She hadn't even realized she was holding her belly protectively when Dr. Farrington, a woman in her early fifties with ash-blond hair and a harried smile, came up beside her. "Another contraction?"

"No. No more contractions. I was just thinking about...her father."

"We all miss Todd a great deal," Dr. Farrington said sympathetically. "I know how hard this must be for you, having the baby without him."

No one knew the real story behind her marriage except for Janetta, and even *she* didn't know all of it. "I'm putting a new life together now," Risa said softly.

"Raising a child as a single parent is challenging."

"It's a challenge I'm ready for." She was certain of that...just as she was certain she'd never completely trust a man again...just as she was certain she'd never marry again.

"I heard Sheriff Blackstone brought you in."

"He lives next door."

"I see."

Risa didn't know exactly what Dr. Farrington saw. If the obstetrician thought she and Simon were involved...the idea was impossible. The black-haired, blue-eyed sheriff had a reputation for being a straight-shooter but a lady's man. She could understand why women were attracted to him in that blue uniform with his broad shoulders, his six-two height and a killer smile that made the set of his jaw not quite so severe. He could probably date absolutely any woman he wanted.

Trying to forget about the man who'd lifted her into his arms with practically no effort at all, she asked her obstetrician, "Am I supposed to keep walking?"

"Just wander around for another fifteen minutes or so. Let Mary take your blood pressure again. But from my examination and the lack of further contractions, I think you'll be going home. This baby's not quite ready to make an appearance."

"If I had *false* labor pains, the real ones must be doozies."

"Your body is readying you for this experience. Listen to it, Risa. Pamper yourself for the next couple of weeks. Will Janetta be home by your due date?"

"She's not sure. But I can always call Lucy or my mother if I need them."

"Good. And," she added with a smile, "I imagine since the sheriff lives next door, you have the best emergency service available. So take advantage of it if you have to. I'm going to go up to OB and check on another of my patients. When I come back down, if there aren't any further developments with you, we'll check you out."

After she put her hand on Risa's shoulder and gave her a motherly squeeze, she headed for the elevator.

Risa sat beside Simon in his SUV, much too aware of his black wavy hair under his Stetson, his strong hands on the wheel, his male scent in the air-conditioned cab. What was wrong with her? She was going to have a baby. Soon, if today was any indication.

"I jumped the gun, didn't I?" he asked, breaking into the silence.

"What do you mean?"

"I shouldn't have rushed you to the hospital. Now you'll have to pay for that emergency room visit—"

"I have good insurance with the school, and I'm finally making a dent in the bills—" She cut off, not really wanting him to know anything about that.

Instead of the bills, he picked up on the first part of her sentence. "You work for a school?"

Although they were neighbors, he probably knew as

little about her as she knew about him. "Yes. I teach at the elementary school. I'm a reading specialist."

He glanced at her as he pulled up in front of Janetta's two-story house. "What does that mean? You help kids who can't read?"

"I help children who have trouble reading. There can be many different reasons for that. I work up plans to help them progress no matter what level they're on."

Switching off the ignition, he studied her for a few moments. "That's an important job."

"Probably as important as what you do," she said with a smile, feeling more comfortable with him now.

"I see the results of what happens when children can't read, quit school and don't have many options. You're on the preventative end. I'm on the cleanup end. I probably don't have to have the patience you do," he added with a knowing look. Then he opened his door and climbed out.

Around to her side of the vehicle before she'd even unfastened her seat belt, he offered, "Let me help you down. That's a high step."

The truth was, Risa wasn't used to a man being so thoughtful. Everything Simon Blackstone had done today had been in consideration of her. Maybe that's why her stomach fluttered whenever she looked into those blue, blue eyes. Maybe that's why when he took both her hands in his to help her down, her pulse raced and she felt his touch all the way to her toes. He was slow to release her hands and when he did, she felt flustered.

"Did your doctor give you any instructions on what to do next?"

"Other than wait, you mean?" Risa asked.

He chuckled. "I guess you need patience even before a baby's born. Do you know the sex?"

"It's a little girl." The tenderness and love she already felt underlied her soft tone. She talked to little Francie every day, played music for her, even read to her.

"Do you have a name picked out?"

"Francesca Marie. I'm going to call her Francie."

"Nice name." Glancing at her house, he asked, "Are you sure you should be alone?"

Her shoulders squared at that. "I'm having a baby, Sheriff. I'm capable of lifting the phone if I need to call for help."

"Unless you're out on the front porch or in the backyard. And the name is Simon, remember? We're neighbors."

They were, and she shouldn't be so defensive. But for two years, Todd had questioned every one of her decisions and made her doubt herself. Now she stood on her own two feet and handled whatever came her way.

"Simon," she repeated, gazing into those blue eyes, feeling almost breathless. "Thank you for helping me this afternoon. But really, I'll be fine. The next time I have a contraction, I'll just breathe through it. This afternoon, I panicked and forgot everything I'd learned."

"What are you going to do about supper?" he asked practically.

"I hadn't thought about it. Maybe some yogurt and a salad."

"That's not enough for two," he scolded.

"I'll eat for two tomorrow."

"When I came home earlier, I was going to change and go to the diner up on Poplar Street for supper. Why don't I go pick up two turkey dinners and then you'll have a hot supper with some substance."

"You're afraid I'm going to have contractions again, aren't you?" she asked, reading the concern under his suggestion.

"I know they call it false labor, but those contractions were preparing you for something."

Suddenly she realized that Simon Blackstone might be the sheriff of Cedar Corners, but he was also a kind man. She couldn't be rude to him or turn him away simply because she got tingles every time she looked at him…or hot flashes any time he touched her.

Besides, she had to admit company would be nice. "A turkey dinner sounds great."

"If you're not starving, I'll grab a shower before I get the dinners."

"I'm not starving. I have fresh lemonade in the fridge. If I put glasses in the freezer, they'll get frosty."

"Rest until I get back," he warned her.

It was more of a suggestion than an order, she told herself. She gave him a smile and a wave, then headed up the curved cement path to the house. This afternoon had unnerved her—the contractions…Simon Blackstone's effect on her. It would take the next half hour for her to find her balance again.

When Simon returned from the diner with two dinners, he wondered what in the hell he was doing. The invitation to Risa to share supper with him had flown out of his mouth before he could catch it. She awakened every protective instinct inside of him, plus a few others. Didn't he know better than to get involved with a woman like her? She was a widow...*and* pregnant. She'd been married to the chief of staff of the hospital and if she ever *did* get involved with a man again, it would be one who was willing to build a picket fence, buy a dog and have umpteen kids.

Simon didn't put much weight in the romantic notion of love and marriage. His mother had loved his no-good father until Dan Blackstone had died in prison. She'd loved him so much that after his death, she'd formed a relationship with vodka instead of her son. Whether she'd been drunk, delusional, or just tired of living in Oklahoma City, she'd given him to his aunt to raise. If that's how love and marriage turned out, he wanted no part of it. He didn't know the first thing about a good family life, how husbands should act or what fathers should be. Why take a chance he'd mess it up?

Two years ago, Renée Barstow, a PR consultant he'd hired for his election had taught him another important life-truth. He'd forgotten his resolve not to get serious, to leave when the sex got too hot or the word commitment came up. She'd been a looker as well as intelligent. They'd been dating three months when the subject of his background arose. As soon as he told her his father had been a convict, she'd stopped returning his calls.

He'd told himself it was better that way. He'd told

himself he was a confirmed bachelor. He'd told himself wedding vows and bridal veils didn't belong in his universe. Yet sometimes in the middle of the night...

When he knocked on the back door, Risa opened it, smiled and invited him inside. That smile of hers did something to him he didn't like very much because he felt out of his depth...intrigued...aroused.

She's pregnant, he repeated to himself for the thousandth time.

"Here's your piping hot turkey dinner, complete with plastic utensils, napkins, and—" he lifted a second bag "—two pieces of Connie's coconut cake. Do you like coconut cake?"

"Sure, but if I eat the turkey dinner I won't have room for it."

"Save it for later," he suggested with a wink. He waited until she sat at the small round maple table with its blue gingham place mats, then he pulled in a chair beside her. He noticed she'd already poured two glasses of lemonade.

As a ceiling fan whirred overhead, Risa produced a ten-dollar bill from the pocket of her bright pink maternity jumper and handed it to him. He asked, "What's this?"

"Dinner. I certainly don't expect you to pay for mine."

There was something in her tone that alerted him this was an issue for her. She was intently serious about paying him and he had the feeling that if he didn't let her, he'd have a battle on his hands.

Sliding his wallet from his cut-off jeans, he took out

the proper change and tucked it into her hand. "I wouldn't want you to overpay." Her fingers were warm, and his sudden gesture caused a flash of awareness in her eyes that made him think that whatever attraction he felt wasn't one-sided.

Pulling her hand from his, she tucked the dollar bills into her pocket. "Do you eat at the diner often?"

He watched her as she opened the bag, handed him one of the plastic containers, and opened her own.

"A few times a week. It's good food. What about you?"

"When Janetta's home, we take turns cooking."

"Her job takes her out of town often?"

"On and off. She's setting up a new office for her company's bank in Tulsa. She travels to different branches, trains new personnel. I miss her when she's gone. She's the one person in my family with respect for my boundaries. She usually doesn't meddle or try to tell me what to do. Do you have any brothers or sisters?"

He took a big bite of turkey, chewed and swallowed. "No. No brothers or sisters. No family."

"I'm sorry," she said as if she couldn't imagine it. "Your parents are both gone?"

"A long time ago. My aunt raised me. About six years ago, she had a stroke and died. That's when I moved here."

"Where did you grow up?"

"Oklahoma City. I was on the police force there when a friend told me the sheriff here would be retiring. I needed a change and it seemed like a good move."

"Janetta said you bought the house next door about a year ago."

"That's right. I decided Cedar Corners was a good place to settle down, at least for now."

Suddenly the expression on Risa's face changed, became strained, and her hand went to her tummy.

"Are you okay?"

"Just a twinge. Nothing like this afternoon. The doctor told me that might happen."

"Maybe you should call your mother or sister. Staying alone might not be such a great idea."

This time her expression was almost fierce. "Sheriff…" She stopped. "Simon, having this baby isn't going to interfere with my judgment. The doctor told me if I start having contractions five minutes apart or less, I should get to the hospital. I'll do that. Until then, I don't need a keeper."

He could see taking care of herself was a big deal for her, and he had to wonder why. Had her family tried to take over her life since her husband had died? "There's something you have to understand, Risa. A pregnant woman brings out protective instincts in a man. I'm sure you *are* fully capable of taking care of yourself. But right now…" His gaze went to her belly. "You shouldn't take any chances."

"I won't," she assured him.

They ate the rest of their dinner in silence.

He finished his, although Risa only ate about half of hers. He remembered her figure before she'd become pregnant. She'd been slender, and actually still was. The weight she'd gained was all concentrated in her belly.

By the time he finished his coconut cake, he knew

he should leave, but he didn't want to. It was an odd feeling, just wanting to sit here with Risa. Usually when he was with a woman, he wanted to be doing something—-hiking, boating, having sex. Having sex with Risa had played like a videotape in his dreams ever since she'd moved in with her sister. But the idea had been ludicrous under the circumstances and still was. He was a bit surprised she hadn't mentioned her husband or how much she missed him with the baby coming. On the other hand, she might not want to talk about something so personal with a stranger.

Risa took a few sips of lemonade and set her glass on the table next to her half-eaten dinner. "Thank you for everything you did for me today. I appreciate it."

Standing, he said, "No thanks necessary."

After she levered herself up from the chair, she looked up at him. "You went beyond the call of duty."

They were standing so close, the material of her jumper almost touched his belt buckle. The scent of her perfume wafted around him in the air-conditioned kitchen. He'd noticed it right away when he'd lifted her into his arms this afternoon. Jasmine. His aunt had grown it on a trellis in the backyard.

Risa wasn't wearing makeup and her natural look got to him almost as much as her smile. If he bent toward her, would she back away?

An Off-Limits sign flashed in his head and he stepped back. Maybe he was putting in too many hours. Maybe he needed a vacation. Maybe he should stop in and enjoy happy hour at the Grand Falloon bar where singles mingled and connected.

"You take care," he said as any neighbor or sheriff would as he stepped away from her and went to the back door.

She nodded and waved as he left, saying, "I will."

Instead of heading for his house, Simon took out his keys and went to the garage at the rear of his yard where he kept his truck. Visiting the Grand Falloon was exactly what he needed. One way or another he'd forget about Risa Parker and everything that had happened this afternoon. A night of dancing to the jukebox with a pretty woman in his arms ought to take care of it.

Chapter Two

Though Simon had intended to have a great time at the Grand Falloon, he hadn't. Instead of dancing with a pretty girl, he'd played cards all night in the back room with two of his deputies and a couple of friends. Not that there hadn't been pretty girls sipping drinks and standing around the jukebox, they just hadn't tempted him tonight.

After all, he'd turned thirty-five last winter. That milestone might have changed his attitude. Getting physical needs met just wasn't the recreation it used to be.

Lowering himself to his sofa, he flicked on the TV but found nothing but infomercials. He was edgy tonight, not ready to go to bed.

Wandering through the kitchen, he opened the back door and stepped out onto his patio. There was a sliver of a moon, and only a few twinkling stars shone. That's probably why he noticed the lights in the house next door. Light spilled out the kitchen window. Upstairs, a yellow glow in a bedroom shone through the slanted blinds. When he had come home from the Grand Falloon, Risa's house had been dark.

He glanced at the luminescent dial of his watch. It was 2 a.m.! Was Risa having contractions again?

There was only one way to find out. If he called and she didn't answer the phone, he'd know she needed help. Impatiently looking up her number in the phone book in the kitchen, he jabbed in the numbers quickly.

She answered on the first ring. "Hello?" It was a husky question, asking who would be calling this time of night.

"It's Simon. I saw your lights on. Are you okay?"

There was a momentary pause. "I haven't had any more contractions. It's just insomnia. For the past two weeks I can't seem to get to sleep at night. I've been catching up on professional journals. When I get bored reading, I make sure the layette's ready for the baby."

"Layette?" He wasn't familiar with terms surrounding babies.

"Playsuits and pajamas, towels and diapers—everything I'll need when I bring her home."

All at once Simon had an idea that would help him keep his eye on Risa and might give her something to do when she couldn't sleep. "Do you want something to think about other than professional journals and layettes?"

This time the pause was longer. "What?" she asked almost warily.

"I'm putting together a public safety campaign for kids. When school opens, I'll be visiting classrooms and talking to them. But I could use a professional consultant. How about we get together and you give me your safety concerns from a teacher's and mom's point of view? You might have suggestions I'd never think of."

She was quiet as she considered it for a little while. "That would give me something to keep me occupied. Would you like me to make notes for us to discuss? I have a laptop and can type them up."

"That's fine. Or you could just jot down a few ideas. I'm sure I'm going to have questions. I've been getting input from the other deputies all week. Maybe we can get together a couple of nights and go over the whole thing."

When she went silent, the stillness lasted for so long, he wasn't sure she hadn't stepped away from the phone. "Risa?"

"I'm here. Do you really need my input on this, or is it your way of watching over me?"

He should have known she'd guess his motives. "Both. I do need a professional's point of view, and I'll also be able to see for myself that you haven't gone into labor and can't reach the phone."

As moments ticked by, he knew she was there and that she was thinking and analyzing, deciding whether or not she was going to let him be a meddling neighbor. Actually he was surprised he was pushing this hard. But the thought of her in labor and alone—

"I'll be your consultant under one condition," she finally responded.

He'd suspected she wouldn't give in easily. "What's the condition?"

"You have to let me cook you supper tomorrow night to repay you for your kindness today."

A protest came to his lips, but he clamped them tight to let her finish.

"And we have to meet on equal terms, professional to professional. You have to promise not to hover."

"I don't hover," he grumbled.

Now she laughed. "Not much. Remember, Simon, I don't need a keeper."

She certainly was touchy about that. "I'm getting the message, Risa. When you go into labor, you're going to drive yourself to the hospital, not even park in the emergency parking area and walk yourself up to the obstetrics unit, all the while breathing however women are supposed to breathe when they're having a baby."

"Exactly," she agreed, a lilt to her tone that told him she was still smiling.

Running his hand through his hair, he smiled, too. "What time tomorrow night?"

"Around six?"

"That sounds good."

"I'll see you tomorrow night, then."

"Good night, Risa." When he hung up the phone, he stared out the window at her house again.

He was not going to get involved with Risa Parker. He was just going to keep his eye on her until her sister got home.

* * *

During the following week or so, Risa consulted with Simon three times about his public safety campaign for schoolchildren. He was organized, direct and willing to listen to her ideas, incorporating them whenever he could. Each time they met, she realized he was checking her out carefully. He asked whether she'd had any more contractions and generally gave her a thorough appraisal. Those blue eyes of his caused shivers even in ninety-degree heat. She knew he was simply looking for signs that she was tired, overdoing it or not eating. The truth was, she felt good and energetic, more so than in the past few weeks.

On Friday evening when they were putting the finishing touches on the activities Simon would be doing with the elementary schoolchildren, he said with a frown, "Now I just wish I had more experience with kids."

When he leaned back in his chair, he looked troubled. They were sitting across from each other at the kitchen table.

"You haven't been around children very much?" she asked, much too aware of his hair-roughed arms crossed on the table, his cutoffs revealing powerful thighs, his hair falling over his brow.

"Not a lot. I'm not on the streets as much as my deputies. I should practice relating to kids before I dive into classrooms."

After a moment of debating with herself, she made a suggestion. "I have an easy solution to that if you're serious."

"What? You know a few kids I can borrow to experiment with?" His smile was crooked and teasing and her stomach somersaulted. Or maybe that was Francie moving around.

She smiled. "In a manner of speaking. You can come with me to my mother's house for dinner on Sunday. My sister Lucy has three children. David's ten, Tanya's six, and Mary Lou is three. Besides, you'll see what I mean about my family taking over my life and why I don't like to call them unless it's absolutely necessary."

After Simon considered her invitation for a long time without saying anything, she continued, "On the other hand, I can see why you wouldn't want to get mixed up with the Lombardi clan, a lasagna dinner and kids who have a little more freedom than they should." With his reputation, an afternoon like she was suggesting might sound boring.

"The kids are wild?" Simon asked curiously.

"No, not wild. It's just that Lucy and Janetta and I were strictly raised. Lucy's gone to the other extreme with her kids. She has a hard time saying no to them."

"Are you sure your family won't mind if you bring along a stranger?"

Risa considered that. Ever since her marriage, she'd stayed away from men. Todd had gotten jealous easily, and after his death… The truth be told, she couldn't imagine ever wanting to date a man again. But she *wasn't* dating Simon. Over the past week though, somehow, he'd become a friend.

"You're not a stranger any more. You're my neighbor and…a friend."

He seemed to absorb that. After a glance at his notes,

he decided. "Dinner with your nieces and nephew could be just the practice I need."

After Simon left, Risa phoned her mother and told her she'd be bringing along a friend to Sunday dinner. Carmen Lombardi didn't seem particularly interested and wanted to talk about the bassinet cover she'd made for Risa's baby, as well as classes Risa, Lucy and her husband Dominic would have to attend before the baby's baptism. Parents and godparents both had to participate in sacramental preparation. By the time Risa got off the phone, bringing along a friend for dinner had been forgotten. But Risa suspected her mother thought she'd be bringing a woman friend. She wouldn't make explanations until she had to.

When Simon came to Risa's front door on Sunday morning around eleven, she'd just gotten home from church. She'd worn a two-piece white maternity dress with short sleeves, a sweetheart neck and blue, yellow, and pink smocking on the bodice.

Simon's gaze took her in with one swift look—from her bangs and hair held back from her face with French braids and tied with a pink ribbon, to her white leather sandals. The sparks in his eyes seemed to start Francie dancing in Risa's tummy like a prima ballerina.

"Do you always dress up for family dinners?" he asked.

"I dressed for Mass. I won't be able to wear this too much longer...I hope."

Today Simon was wearing black casual slacks and a black-and-gray plaid, Western-cut shirt. She was used to seeing him either in his uniform, or jeans and a

T-shirt. His jawline, which usually started to stubble by evening, was freshly shaven. She liked his aftershave. It was lemony with a touch of pine.

As he escorted her to his truck, he asked, "Your mother didn't mind that you were bringing somebody to dinner?"

Risa shrugged. "Not at all."

However that wasn't the impression Simon got when Mrs. Lombardi greeted the two of them in her living room. Her mouth rounded in surprise and then she scrutinized him up and down as if she expected him to steal the silver candelabra on the mantel.

Simon figured the direct approach was best and extended his hand. "Sheriff Simon Blackstone."

"Sheriff Blackstone?" she repeated with a really troubled expression now. "I've heard several rumors about you." She looked at Risa.

"I'm sure you've heard that he's a wonderful sheriff," Risa said quickly.

"Yes, among other things," Mrs. Lombardi admitted with narrowed eyes. "Have you known each other long?"

"He's my next-door neighbor," Risa answered again. "I had false labor pains last week and he took me to the hospital to get them checked out."

"False labor pains. Lucy!" she called to her other daughter in the kitchen. "Did you hear that? I didn't think there *were* such things." She put her arms around Risa's shoulders. "Are you all right? Should you be in bed?"

At that moment, Simon began to understand what

Risa meant about her mother overreacting. Still...Risa seemed to take it all in stride as her sister joined them from the kitchen and clucked over her, too. After Risa allayed their many concerns, she showed Simon to the kitchen that smelled of wonderful aromas.

Out back, Lucy's three children were setting up a water sprinkler with their father. A few minutes later introductions were made again there, and Dominic connected Simon's name with his occupation immediately.

Risa's brother-in-law had an easy smile, dark brown hair and a friendly manner. "I voted for you," he said proudly.

Little Mary Lou took hold of her father's leg and peeked out from behind his plaid Bermuda shorts.

From the porch, Carmen Lombardi called, "Dinner's ready. Come now. We don't want anything to get cold."

"As if it could on a day like this," Dominic mumbled under his breath.

The temperature was already in the high nineties and destined to go higher. Simon wondered how Risa was going to hold up. Although there were room air conditioners in the older house, the kitchen was still warm from the heat of the oven.

When Risa had answered her door earlier, he'd been bowled over by her. She'd looked as fresh as a spring day. Her cheeks were a little pinker now but she absolutely glowed, and he didn't think he'd ever seen a woman who looked more beautiful...pregnant or not! That thought threw him. A few of the faces and figures of women he'd dated whom he'd considered model-perfect flashed through his mind in fast succession. None of them could hold a candle to Risa's pure beauty.

At dinner, Simon and Dominic talked about the new computer system the sheriff's office was installing.

Mrs. Lombardi was dishing out a second wedge of the lasagna onto Simon's plate when she remarked, "As sheriff, you probably know most of the town."

From what he'd observed already, he guessed Carmen had a point to this conversation. He'd find out soon enough what it was. "I don't know everyone. Just the folks I run into—and then of course, the ones who get in trouble."

Dominic and Lucy laughed, but Carmen didn't crack a smile.

Instead, she placed the lasagna turner upside down on the pan so it wouldn't stain the white tablecloth. "Did you know Dr. Todd Parker?"

With a quick glance at Risa, Simon noticed the pink leave her cheeks. "No, I didn't, Mrs. Lombardi. I was called to the scene the night of the accident, though. I'm sorry it happened."

Risa's mother had a pained expression. "We all were. He was such a wonderful man. *So* well respected. And he gave generously to the community, too."

As chief of staff at the hospital, Dr. Todd Parker had drawn the kind of salary Simon would never see. But for him, police work wasn't about money. It was about giving back and becoming the man his father had never been.

"It's such a shame Todd will never see his daughter," Carmen went on, her voice breaking.

"Mama," Risa murmured.

"Oh, I know you're still grieving, too, honey."

Lucy hopped up from her seat then and looked around the table. "I think it's time to refill the bread basket. There's more garlic bread, isn't there, Mama?"

The tension that had cropped up around the table seemed over the top. It was only natural for relatives to want to talk about lost loved ones. Maybe Risa wanted to keep her grief private and they all knew that, except for her mother. On the other hand, he realized Carmen Lombardi had brought up Todd Parker to make a statement about the type of man her daughter deserved— educated, a leader in the community, earning a huge salary.

After the main course, Carmen served dessert. The cannoli she'd made were delicious and Simon told her so.

Cocking her head, she studied him as if gauging his sincerity. Then she nodded and murmured, "Thank you."

Risa was pulling some kind of kids' toy from a bag when Simon found her in her mother's living room a short time later. Everyone else had gone outside after they'd helped in the clean-up process to watch the kids enjoy the sprinkler. "I wondered where you disappeared to."

"Lucy brought some things for me to look through in case I want them for Francie."

Already, Simon felt as if he was beginning to know Risa quite well. "Is that the only reason you're in here?"

"I just needed a few moments to myself," she murmured.

He looked down at the toy in her hands. Maybe the

subject of Todd Parker at dinner had brought back too much sadness. At the thought of the man, Simon felt jealousy he didn't understand. Jealousy wasn't an emotion he was familiar with. Instead of examining it, he took the toy from Risa. "What is this?"

When she smiled up at him, the urge to kiss her was so strong he could hardly stifle it.

"It's a busy box." One by one she flipped up a lever, pressed a button that squeaked, turned a handle in a circle and slid a little blue box to the right. A cartoon character popped up with each of her manipulations.

"Doesn't that scare kids?" he asked.

She laughed. "Nope. It teaches eye-hand coordination, cause and effect. This is an older version. The new ones light up and play music, too."

Simon shook his head and bent to lay the toy on the sofa once more. Then he straightened. They were standing very close. The scent of jasmine surrounded him. He'd tried to play the role of a friendly neighbor today, but it just wasn't working. His elbow grazed hers. He saw the same startle of awareness in her eyes that kicked him in the gut.

Reaching out, he brushed a tendril of hair from her cheek. "Did I tell you how pretty you look today?"

Ducking her head, she murmured, "Simon…"

It was some kind of warning, but he didn't heed it. Sliding his thumb under her chin, he tipped her head up. "What's the matter? Don't you think pregnant women can look pretty?"

"I feel fat," she admitted with a self-conscious laugh. Touching Risa gave Simon pleasure. He realized how much he wanted to touch her more. Unable to resist, he rested his hand on her shoulder. The cotton puffed sleeve of her dress felt all together feminine. Everything about Risa was feminine. Stepping in a little closer, he knew it was a bold move since they were in her mother's living room, but he didn't seem to have common sense where Risa was concerned. Impulses struggled to overpower self-control.

As she stared up at him mesmerized, his fingers slid across her shoulder, and he touched the delicate pearl stud at her ear. He felt her tremble. What about this woman got to him so?

"Simon," she said again. This time there was anticipation in her tone. There was a little catch that told him she was as affected being this close to him as he was being close to her.

Suddenly there was the opening and shutting of the back door in the kitchen. Lucy's voice called into the living room, "I'm getting some lemonade. Do you want any?"

"That sounds great," Simon called back. "We'll be right out."

Before he could say a word to Risa or touch her again, she moved away, busily stowing away the busy box.

The moment had been shattered. Simon felt the loss of it at a deep place inside he hadn't even known was there.

A few minutes later, he was in the yard trying to get a handle on the kids, wondering why David didn't want to come anywhere near him.

Lucy joined him by the swing set under the shade of

a tall elm. She was a good four inches taller than Risa, pleasantly plump, her hair lighter. "Risa told me you thought you needed practice with kids before you went into the schools to try to teach them safety rules. Anytime you want to borrow my three for the day, just let me know."

He laughed. "They *are* energetic." They were squealing and yelling as they ran in and out of the water in their bathing suits.

"It's not so hard to relate to kids," she commented, serious now. "For instance, if you ask Tanya about her gymnastic classes, she'll talk your ear off. The secret with all children is tapping into their world."

"That makes sense."

After a short pause, Lucy tackled the next subject she apparently wanted to discuss. "Risa told me you check on her now and then, and that's how you became friends."

Simon wondered if Lucy had given Risa the third degree. "She worried me when she had those contractions."

"And you being her neighbor and all, you just thought you had to watch over her."

Simon remained silent.

But that didn't stop Lucy. "My mother pretty much sees what she wants to see whether that concerns her own life or Risa's or Todd Parker's."

This time Simon couldn't stay his curiosity. "There was another side to Risa's husband that he didn't show your mother?"

"I'll say. He was *so* generous that he left Risa in

enough debt she had to move in with Janetta. Mama doesn't know that. Todd wasn't what he seemed. I don't think any of us know the whole story except Risa, and she's not talking."

As Simon considered that, Lucy confessed, "I just thought you should know."

Although Lucy moved away and went in the house again, her comments stuck with Simon as he tossed a ball to a dripping little Mary Lou, then asked Tanya about her gymnastics and was regaled with her experiences on the gymnastics team. After those successes, he tried to engage David in a conversation. But the boy was monosyllabic and soon found an excuse to go inside, too.

As the day became hotter, the kids changed out of their suits and everyone found a place inside in the much cooler house. As Risa spoke with her family, Simon noticed she skated on the surface of her life. She didn't talk about anything important, and most of the time, although Carmen, Lucy and Dominic had strong opinions, Risa didn't express hers. He knew she had them because she didn't hesitate to share them with him. Yet there was a certain reserve about her when she interacted with him, too. Granted, they'd only really known each other for about ten days. Still...

When they left Carmen Lombardi's house, Risa was quiet and looked tired. Simon imagined the day had taken its toll. They drove the short distance home in silence, and he insisted on walking Risa to her door. "Are you feeling okay?"

"As okay as I can with a seven-pound bowling ball

in my tummy. Do you feel your class in Kids 101 was worthwhile?"

He had to smile at her description of the afternoon. "I didn't learn much about ten-year-olds. Does David always keep to himself?"

"He's one of those boys who has everything from a computer to a 26-inch TV in his bedroom. He's quiet when he's around adults, but around kids his own age, I hear he can be a terror. His teacher called Lucy and Dom for a conference more than once last year."

Ever since summer started, there'd been sporadic vandalism around Cedar Corners. Simon and his deputies attributed it to teenagers with nothing better to do. He hoped David wasn't headed in that direction.

"Your sister and her husband are friendly. I can see that your mom likes to interfere. Are the two of you close?"

"I love Mama dearly," Risa said with a sigh. "She'd do anything for me and I'd do anything for her. But she's very rigid. Both my parents were. When my dad was alive, she believed her job was to cater to his every need and he believed she should do just that. After Dad died, Mama wore black and didn't go out for a year, not even to the grocery store. Lucy and I were in high school then and we took care of all that."

"And Janetta?"

"She was at college. She's a lot more vocal with Mama than Lucy and I are. My mom lives in her own world with her own values and heaven forbid if we don't agree with her. What about your parents? What were they like?"

Regretting his questions now, Simon should have realized this discussion would eventually lead here. Or maybe he realized he'd brought it up on purpose. He was who he was and if Risa couldn't accept that, he guessed she'd have to find someone else to watch over her until her sister returned home. "My family was as dysfunctional as one could get. My father wrote bad checks, was arrested for fraud and eventually assault. He died in prison when a fight broke out."

As Risa's eyes went wide, Simon continued anyway. "My mother loved my father so much that she started drinking and decided taking care of a kid just wasn't her thing. So she left me with my aunt. A few years later, we got word that she died of pneumonia."

Risa was silent for a few moments and then she clasped his forearm. "I'm sorry, Simon."

Suddenly the phone began ringing inside.

"That's probably Janetta," Risa murmured.

If Risa needed a getaway to escape this conversation, he'd give it to her. "Go answer it. If you talk to your mom again, thank her for dinner for me."

As the phone beckoned to Risa again, she hesitated a moment, but then she nodded and went inside.

Simon strode to his house wondering if the friendship that had begun with Risa was now over.

Risa's back pain started around 9 p.m. She thought she was just tired from the day. While she took a shower, she remembered again everything Simon had told her about his family. There had been an almost defiant look in his eyes when he'd related his background, and she didn't quite understand that. Did he think it would make a difference in what she thought of him?

She knew better than anyone that a background shaped you, but it didn't make you who you were. You did that yourself. She was in the process now of re-making herself into a woman she could respect and admire. Before Todd, she hadn't thought much about who she wanted to be. Now she did. She would learn independence and self-sufficiency no matter what the cost, and she'd never take orders from a man again...or trust one. Todd had put on a charming face before he'd married her and let the facade drop afterward. He'd shown one side of himself to his social circle and his colleagues...and another to her.

Looking back over the past ten days or so, Risa realized she'd fallen into this friendship with Simon because he seemed to be exactly what he said he was. She recognized fake smiles now, as well as flattery that wasn't sincere. She recognized an attitude that said, *I'm much better than you are and I know a lot more.* She hadn't sensed any of that in Simon.

After she slipped on her nightgown, she decided to make sure she'd unpacked everything she'd bought for the baby. There still might be new clothes stored in the old chest in the nursery. The windows in the baby's room faced Simon's house. Lights blazed in his downstairs, and she wondered if he was watching TV or sitting outside on his patio.

She *shouldn't* be wondering.

She was about to have a baby and Simon was just keeping an eye on her until Janetta returned. After that, they might not even have a friendship, simply wave hello and goodbye when they came and went. She'd be too busy with Francie to think about a few tingles, a few skipped heartbeats or Simon's smile when he teased her.

Attempting to dismiss the man from her thoughts, she let the nursery's bright decor excite her as it always did. She'd wallpapered the room in a small, simple white-and-green pattern. The wide border near the ceiling carried those colors and pictures of kittens sleeping and playing. The crib and changing table were a light oak and supplies were stacked everywhere. A shopping bag sat by the changing table on the floor, and she remembered it held cotton playsuits she'd bought on sale last week. It was still early. She'd run a load of laundry with some of her things, too.

As she leaned over to pick up a bag, she was stunned by the contraction that overtook her. Fighting against it, she struggled to stay upright and held onto the table. This contraction was much more severe than the one she'd had on the porch. Could it be false labor again?

She hardly regained her breath from the first contraction when the second one hit, coming about two minutes later. This time she doubled over and then went down on the floor on her hands and knees. This had to be real!

On the floor, she remembered what she'd learned and breathed through the contraction. Then she timed the interval until the next one. Two minutes later, the pain gripped her again and she realized she needed to get help. At two minutes apart, she might not even have time to get to the hospital.

She couldn't have a baby this quickly, could she?

Biding her time, breathing as best she could and trying to remain calm, as soon as the next contraction ended she pushed herself up and hurried to her bedroom. If she could just reach the phone on the nightstand…

She'd written Simon's number on the tablet there. Now, just as the next contraction hit, she jabbed in the numbers on the cordless phone. Pain as severe as a few minutes before tore through her body.

Her voice shaking, she said, "Simon," when he picked up.

"Risa, what's wrong?"

"Hold on," she implored as the pain made her clench her teeth and she waited for it to pass.

"Risa?"

"Contractions…have started again. They're two minutes apart. I don't know if I should try to get to the hospital."

"I'll call 911. Are your doors locked?"

"Yes. But there's a key in a fake rock right behind the latticework under the back porch. It's in the left corner. I'd come down—"

She didn't think even two minutes had passed this time as the cramping stole her breath and she sank down onto the bed.

"Don't move," he ordered. "I'll be right there."

Fear washed through Risa along with the pain as she waited for Simon…and prayed.

Chapter Three

Simon let himself in the back door, ran to the steps and took them two at a time. In the doorway to Risa's bedroom, he stopped.

Beside the bed on the floor, she'd curled her legs up. In her hands were some kind of beads.

Striding toward her, striving for the calm he was used to pulling on like an overcoat, he crouched down beside her. "Are you all right?"

She held out the beads that were blue crystal with silver links. "My rosary fell off the nightstand. I needed them. I—" She wrapped her arms around herself as pain gripped her and she held onto the rosary as if it were a lifeline.

"Squeeze my hands," he ordered her, hoping that would help.

Taking hold of his hands, she compressed her lips and her eyes showed the pain she wasn't expressing.

"Scream if you have to."

She shook her head as the contraction ebbed. Finally she took a huge breath. "Screaming takes energy and I'm going to need all the energy I have."

"I called for an ambulance but they're already out on a run. Come on, let me get you in bed. We might have to deliver this baby ourselves."

Her head snapped up and her eyes locked to his. "Ourselves? Do you know how to deliver a baby?"

Scooping her up into his arms, he gently deposited her on the bed. "I had medical training in the academy that included emergency childbirth. Mostly the manual says you just have to let nature take its course."

He could see the worry in her eyes that it might take the *wrong* course.

After pushing her hair away from her face, she rested her hand on her tummy. "Thank goodness I took classes so I can do this naturally. Maybe the contractions will last longer than we think. Maybe they'll stop again. Maybe the ambulance will get here."

But just as she finished her sentence, pain racked her again, building in intensity until it eventually ebbed away once more.

Hating to leave her, he knew he had to prepare for this birth. "Can you get through a couple of the contractions without me? I need to get a few things together."

She held onto the rosary beads tightly. "I'll manage. What do you need?"

"Clean towels. I have to boil scissors and some shoestrings."

She pointed across the room to the foot of the flowered chair where her sneakers lay. "Use my shoelaces. Towels are in the cupboard under the sink in the bathroom. There's a teakettle on the stove for boiling water."

Bending to her, he brushed her damp hair from her brow. "It's going to be okay, Risa. If you can manage it between contractions, call your doctor. Maybe we can get somebody to consult with on the phone."

After he handed her the cordless phone, he grabbed her shoes and went to the bathroom for the towels.

Ten minutes later he was back upstairs. Risa had pulled the pink-and-yellow flowered spread off the bed and flung it to the side.

"My water broke," she said, obviously distressed. "I feel as if I have to push."

He knew what he had to do next, but he didn't know how Risa was going to react.

Her shoestrings floated in the sterile water in a measuring cup, and he set it on the nightstand. "I have to look, Risa, and see what's happening. If the baby's head is there, then it's time to push."

Although her cheeks were already flushed, they turned redder. "I'll...I'll imagine you're my doctor."

Right. While she was imagining that, *he* was going to pretend she was some woman he'd found along the side of the road who was about to deliver. Somehow he had to remove himself from what was happening here and try not to personally react to any of it.

"All right then," he stated matter-of-factly, trying to

keep his tone clinical. "Let me help you down to the edge of the bed. You can prop your feet on the foot-board."

Curving his arm around her shoulders, he helped her inch down. When she turned her head to look at him, her face was very close to his.

No matter what he told himself, the tight tugging low in his body reminded him this was Risa. Her cotton nightgown lay demurely over her breasts but he could see their outline, could see their shape. Red-hot images raced through his mind, but he shut them off.

As soon as he'd helped Risa to the foot of the bed and thrown a towel over the footboard, he covered her with an afghan that had been tossed over the back of a chair and stacked pillows under her head. Her dark brown eyes watched his every movement. Sometimes he thought he still saw wariness there.

"Did you get hold of your doctor?"

"She's supposed to be calling me back, or at least that's what the answering service said."

When Simon lifted the afghan, his gut tightened. "I can see the head, Risa. Next contraction, you'd better push."

The phone rang then and just as another contraction hit Risa, Simon grabbed it and held it between his chin and shoulder. "Simon Blackstone here. I can see the head. Tell me what to do."

The doctor didn't even tell him her name, she just said matter-of-factly, "Encourage Risa to push until the shoulders are out. Don't panic if it doesn't happen with the first contraction, but do urge her on so you can try and do it quickly."

The doctor's words set the pace.

Simon set the phone on the floor and locked his gaze to Risa's. Pulling a towel into his hands, he ordered, "Next contraction, push for all you're worth. Let's get this baby born."

This would be easier for Risa if he was a complete stranger because, although she might deny it, he knew she felt the sparks zipping between them every time they touched or looked at each other as much as he did. However, right now awkwardness shadowed everything else. He wished he could hold her hand through this process, but he couldn't do that if he had to catch the baby.

When Simon's gaze met Risa's, he felt connected to her in a way he'd never felt connected to a woman before. "It's going to be all right. Your little girl wants to make her entrance so let's get her into your arms."

As a fresh contraction tensed Risa's body, she seemed to embrace it for all she was worth. There was determination on her face and a wealth of emotion Simon couldn't decipher. Working with her body, Risa pushed with all her might. She pushed and pushed...

Simon had seen and felt a lot in his thirty-five years. He was jaded and hardened to the nastier side of life. He'd seen some goodness, too, but that was rare and therefore precious. As Francesca Marie Parker slid into his toweled hands, as he cleared her mouth with his finger, heard her cry, and wiped her little face more gently than he'd ever wiped anything in his life, he felt and saw and held a miracle that rocked him to his core.

Slipping the afghan from Risa with no awkwardness

now, being careful with the umbilical cord, he carefully handed Risa her baby.

Tears slid down her face as she held little Francie. When Risa's dark brown eyes met his, he knew he'd never forget this moment for as long as he lived.

"I don't know how to thank you, Simon," she murmured as she held her baby close.

He could hear a siren. The ambulance was finally on its way.

"You did all the work," he reminded her gruffly.

Watching Risa and her baby nestled on her breasts unsettled Simon in a way he didn't understand.

After he turned away from her, and the event that they'd shared that seemed even more intimate than having sex with a woman, he headed for the doorway. "The paramedics will be here in a couple of minutes. I'll go downstairs and let them in. They can take over from here."

It wasn't in Simon's nature not to see a situation through. But as he stood in Risa's hospital room an hour and a half later, surrounded by Carmen Lombardi, Lucy and Dominic, along with nurses and doctors who knew Risa as well as her deceased husband, he decided it was time to get out of Dodge.

"Doctor Parker would have been so proud," a young blond nurse remarked as she looked down at Francie in her crib next to Risa's bed.

"He certainly would have," Carmen agreed, beaming. "She's the most beautiful child in the whole world."

"My three were the most beautiful children in the whole world," Lucy teased.

Frustrated, Simon checked his watch. He hadn't had two minutes alone with Risa since the paramedics had made an appearance. He'd phoned her sister Lucy as soon as he'd arrived at the hospital. While Risa's doctor checked her out and the pediatrician examined the baby, Carmen, Lucy and Dominic had filed into the waiting room, concerned, chattering and overjoyed.

Simon stepped up beside Risa's bed once more. "I'm going to leave so you can get some rest." He hoped it was a broad hint to her family that they should do the same.

Inching up higher in the bed, Risa smiled at him. "I don't know how to say thank-you, Simon. If it hadn't been for you, I don't know what would have happened."

Her family was listening and watching intently.

"I just happened to be at the right place at the right time. Fortunately, everything went smoothly."

He felt as if he were saying goodbye to Risa and he probably was. Her husband had given her a big house in the right part of town, a fancy car and probably anything else she wanted...in spite of the bills Lucy had revealed Parker had left. Simon would never be in Todd Parker's league, not in salary, not in blue-blooded background. Besides that, now that Risa had a baby, a man would probably be the last thing on her agenda, especially one who only wanted a torrid affair.

"Did you call Janetta?" he asked.

"Lucy did. She said she'd be home next week. Dr. Farrington said I can take Francie home tomorrow."

"That soon?"

"I'd rather be at home with her. I doubt if I'll get much rest here. At home I can settle in."

"If you need anything..." he offered.

Carmen cut in, "She can call us. Thank you for helping tonight, Sheriff, but I don't think there'll be any more emergencies."

"What Mama means," Risa explained apologetically, "is that I won't take advantage of you being my neighbor again. But you're welcome to visit whenever you'd like."

Simon figured Risa was just being polite, and he addressed her mother. "Mrs. Lombardi, it's my job to be available to any citizen in Cedar Corners who needs me. Risa needed me. But I'm sure now she'll rely on her family and your advice as Francie grows."

When he turned his focus to Risa again, the joy he'd seen on her face when he'd handed her Francie was still there. She looked absolutely beautiful. Before he told her so and bent down to put a kiss on her forehead, he'd better leave. He hated the idea of saying goodbye, yet it was necessary.

As he wished her and her family good-night, he thought again about holding Risa's baby at the moment of birth, the expression of pure love on her face, and he knew he wouldn't have missed tonight for anything.

When Lucy brought Risa home from the hospital the following day, it was late afternoon. Checking out and preparing Francie for her trip home had taken more time than they'd expected.

Lucy was glancing at her watch every two minutes. "I have to pick up David and Tanya from their music lessons."

While Risa settled Francie in the bassinet in the living room, Lucy ran upstairs. A few moments later, she was coming down the steps in a hurry, her arms filled with disposable diapers, baby wipes, towels and some baby clothes.

"What are you doing?" Risa asked, looking down at her baby, wondering how soon she would want to eat. She'd latched onto Risa's breast like a pro last night as well as this morning and the nurse didn't think nursing would be a problem.

"If you can't do the steps for a week and you're sleeping on the sofa, that means you're going to need everything down here."

"I have what I need down here," she said quietly. "I have extra of everything in the pantry closet. Really, Lucy, if you need to pick up David and Tanya, just go ahead. We'll be fine."

Lucy dumped everything she'd brought downstairs onto the sofa. "You think it's going to be easy caring for a baby. Well, it's not. Even with Dom's help, I reached the end of my rope lots of days."

"You have three," Risa said with a smile.

"One's plenty when they're crying." Lucy waved at Francie in the bassinet. "Just because she *looks* like an angel, doesn't mean she *is*."

Risa had to laugh at that. "I know raising a child is going to be hard work, but I'm up to it. I've wanted a baby for a long time. You know that."

Immediately Lucy stopped stacking the items on the sofa and looked at her sister. "Yes, I do. I also know if Todd was still around, he wouldn't have been much help. He wasn't that type of man."

Often Risa had thought about confiding in Lucy, as she had Janetta, but she felt ashamed of the dent Todd had made in her spirit. More than that, she felt weak that she hadn't made an attempt to change everything sooner. Maybe if she had, he wouldn't have died. That guilt woke her at times in the middle of the night.

"Thanks for bringing me home today. I really will be fine. All I have to do is feed Francie, change her, and hold her."

Lucy rolled her eyes. "If only it was that easy." Then a sly smile crossed her face. "You can always call the sheriff if you need help."

"I won't be calling Simon."

"Why not? Tall, dark, and handsome. He'd be at the top of my list if *I* was single."

"I'm not interested, Lucy."

"Don't try to fool me. There's something going on between the two of you. I can feel it."

"I think your senses are just overloaded with the heat. Simon helped me when he thought I needed help."

"You called him when you started having contractions."

"I had seen his lights were still on and I knew he could probably get me help the fastest."

Propping her hands on her hips, Lucy didn't buy that reasoning. "I say it's more than that. I say on some level you trust that man."

Lucy couldn't be more wrong. She might have depended on Simon to get emergency services there quickly, but as far as ever trusting a man again, she doubted if she could. She'd fallen in love with Todd, and she'd been wrong about him. Naive and relatively inexperienced, she hadn't seen through his practiced charm. She hadn't realized until it was too late that he showed an easy, friendly nature to the outside world but wanted to control everything in his universe, especially her. It was an old story, she knew. Now she understood better how women got swallowed up, probably married a man expecting the best and not expecting her self-esteem to be destroyed bit by bit. Risa's work had given her the confidence she'd needed to make the right choices. Thank goodness she'd defied Todd on that in spite of her background telling her to give in to him and let him rule their home.

Her statement made, Lucy moved to Risa's kitchen and opened her refrigerator. "You have a few things in here. I'll go grocery shopping tomorrow and stock up for you."

Risa knew she wouldn't be able to drive for at least two weeks. "Thanks, I'd appreciate that. I don't need a lot—bread, milk, yogurt, frozen vegetables, maybe some chicken pieces and fresh greens." Since she was breast-feeding, she had to be careful with her diet.

"You eat like a mouse. I'll make some casseroles and bring them over, too."

"Lucy..." She knew her sister meant well. "I can take care of myself."

Frowning, Lucy closed the refrigerator. "Ever since Todd died, you've been on a mission to prove to everyone you don't need anyone's help. Get over it, Risa. We all need help sometimes."

"I understand that. But Todd—" She cut off her

words and sighed. "I need to know I can stand on my own two feet. I need to know I'm a strong independent woman who can take care of herself. Don't you ever want to feel that power?"

After Lucy thought about it, she smiled. "I feel that kind of power when I go shopping. I don't need it any other time." She became serious again. "I know your marriage to Todd wasn't a good thing. You became more reserved…more quiet. What was going on?"

After a few moments of hesitation, Risa decided, "It doesn't matter now."

Lucy pursed her lips and went silent, but not for long. "Did he hit you?" she asked, astonishing Risa.

"No! Honestly, Lucy, he didn't."

"What *did* he do?" her sister prompted. "Something about your marriage changed you."

Closing her eyes, Risa finally admitted, "He just had this way of questioning everything I did. And there was this anger inside of him that scared me." She went silent again.

"Are you ever going to tell me the whole thing?"

"No. Because all of it is over."

"Mama's made it worse by putting Todd on a pedestal, hasn't she?"

"She liked Todd."

"Mmm. All right. I can see you're not going to tell me more. I'm going to let the subject drop because I have to pick up the kids."

Risa crossed to her sister and hugged her. "Thanks for bringing me home."

"You're welcome. If you need anything, pick up that

phone and call me. Or Simon," she added with an imp-
ish smile.

Risa was still shaking her head when Lucy closed the
door behind her.

It was almost 8 p.m. when Simon came to Risa's
back door. He was carrying something, but she didn't
have time to see what it was. Francie was crying in the
living room even though she had just finished nursing.
Risa was hoping a diaper change might make a difference.

As she grabbed a diaper from the pantry closet, she
motioned Simon to come in.

He followed Risa into the living room, but when he
saw Francie, her little face red from crying, her hands
waving in the air, he stopped.

"What's wrong?" he yelled over the squall.

"I don't know." Risa removed Francie's diaper and
slid another underneath her. "I already fed her. She
even burped. If she keeps this up, she'll make herself
sick." Attaching the diaper in record time, Risa lifted
her little bundle to her shoulder, patting her daughter's
back. None of it comforted the baby.

As Risa walked back and forth across the room, she
asked Simon, "What do you have there?"

"Something for Francie. Think she'll like it?" He
held the stuffed toy out to Risa. It was a gray lamb with
curly fur and a pink ribbon around its neck.

"It's adorable!" Risa took the toy from him and
brushed it along Francie's cheek. "See? Here's your
first stuffed animal. Isn't it cute?"

Francie didn't care about the lamb or anything else. She just kept crying.

"Are you going to call the doctor?" Simon called.

"Not until I've tried everything." Dropping the lamb onto the sofa, she crossed to him. "Can you hold her for a minute?"

The expression on Simon's face was priceless, and Risa suddenly realized he'd probably never held a baby before Francie's birth. "All you have to do is make sure her head is supported," Risa advised him.

"Are you sure you want me to do this? Maybe you could just lay her in her bed."

"She doesn't seem to like it there. If you could just hold her, I'll find a pacifier. I haven't tried that yet."

Simon's expression became a study in determination as his large hands slid under Francie. Risa could feel their roughness against her skin. Their hair-roughened backs brushed against her palms, and she felt that now-recognizable shiver run down her spine. Ignoring it, she watched Simon as he gingerly placed Francie on his shoulder. She was still crying, but not quite as loudly.

"She likes you. She's better already." Risa rushed to the kitchen to find the pacifier she'd washed earlier in the day, trying to distract herself from the sight of her baby girl against Simon's strong broad shoulder.

When she returned to the living room, she crossed to the sofa. "Let's try the car seat." It was sitting on the sofa, padded with pictures of dogs and cats and ducks.

Simon carried Francie to it. "Any special way I should do this?"

He was talking about the transfer from his shoulder

to the car seat and Risa had to smile. "Just keep your hand at the back of her head and her shoulders, and do it gently."

Little Francie looked up at Simon with wide dark eyes as he settled her amidst the printed animals. "It's going to take her a while to grow into that."

"She'll probably grow faster than I want her to." Risa offered the pacifier to her daughter.

At first Francie spit it out, but then Risa offered it again, wiggled it around, and Francie finally took it, sucking contentedly.

"That's all it takes?" Simon asked, amazed.

"Babies' needs are simple ones." Risa looked down at her daughter, brushed her fine brown hair across her forehead, praying she could always meet Francie's needs so easily.

Then she picked up Simon's lamb, ran her fingers over the soft fur, its pink-satin ribbon, and placed it next to Francie where she could see it. "I'm sure this is going to be one of her favorite toys."

"She have a room full of them yet?"

"Not yet. When Mama came to visit, she brought a few." Risa gestured to the blocks, a ball that played music and lit up, according to its cardboard wrapping, and a few books that were sitting on the coffee table.

"I saw your mother leave earlier. I bet she wanted to hold Francie the whole time she was here."

"You're right about that. I think Francie got overtired. Maybe she'll sleep a few hours at a stretch and I can get a nap."

"A nap? How about a night's sleep?"

"I don't think that's going to happen for a few weeks. Maybe longer. Lucy's Mary Lou didn't sleep through the night until she was three months old."

Simon approached her then. He was wearing khaki shorts and a red polo shirt and had never look sexier. After supper Risa had slipped into a royal blue, silky caftan that made feeding the baby easier. Now she felt a bit self-conscious.

Simon looked at her as if he were appraising her body without the baby. She had seven more pounds to lose and didn't know how long it would take.

"How are you feeling?" His blue eyes said he wanted an honest answer.

"Not too bad considering I had a baby yesterday."

"Did you sleep last night?" His voice was husky and low and trilled along her nerve endings.

"Some. But I wanted to make sure Francie had a good start to nursing, so I was awake on-and-off all night. That's the way it's going to be."

"You'll be exhausted," he said practically.

"I don't need much sleep."

"Everyone needs sleep. Were you really going to try to get a nap now?"

Just looking at Simon was an exciting journey. His high forehead with a lock of black hair falling across it, his defined cheekbones, his dark jawline, all entranced her. "I can nap later if you'd like something to drink."

Tearing his gaze from hers, he looked down at Francie. "I think you'd better take the opportunity to rest while you can. I wanted to stop in and…" He paused.

"It's funny," he said. "Watching Francie come into this world, being the first person to hold her, I feel connected to her in some way."

Whenever Risa thought about Simon delivering, then handing her her baby, tears came to her eyes. It was a moment she'd never forget. It sounded as if it were a moment *he* wouldn't forget, either.

The current zipping between them almost took her breath away. The intense look in his eyes practically stopped her heart. She was so aware of the maleness of him, a sensual pull toward him that she'd never felt with any man. Simon was so virile, so strong, so...everything male. And a few months ago, that would have made her run in the other direction. But getting to know him this past week had lowered her defenses...watching him with her daughter just now had lowered them even further.

When Simon bent his head, Risa knew what was going to happen. She could have shifted away. She could have turned her head. She could have dropped down on the sofa beside her daughter. But she didn't. She wanted to face whatever this electricity was with Simon and then deal with it.

As his lips covered hers, they were firm, demanding and masterful. For a moment, she felt a rush of panic. Then that panic dissolved into sensations so intoxicatingly exciting, so sweetly sensual, she couldn't imagine missing any part of this extraordinary kiss.

Simon didn't hesitate to push his tongue into her mouth, and she could tell he was experienced. She could tell he was hungry, too, yet holding the hunger in check. Now she did panic as he awakened needs and feelings that were shaking her world.

Bringing her hands to his chest, she broke away from him and stepped back.

His expression was pained. "I've wanted that for a long time, but I'm not sure you have. You're still grieving. You've just had Parker's baby."

How could she tell him the grief was mixed up with confusion and regret and guilt? How could she tell him that Todd's baby seemed to be more Simon's baby which was absolutely ridiculous! How could she tell him that the trust she'd placed in vows and her husband had been broken by him in so many ways that she might never be able to depend on anyone again?

She didn't really know Simon, and she couldn't tell him any of it.

When she didn't deny what he'd suggested, his expression became grim. "Let's just forget that ever happened."

Maybe Simon would forget, but she knew she never would. She wouldn't forget anything about this week or his part in it, but it would be better if she let him walk out of her life. "Thanks for everything you've done for me."

He nodded to Francie who was sleeping soundly now. "Get some sleep. I'll let myself out and lock the door."

A few moments later when Risa heard the door close, tears came to her eyes. *Hormones,* she told herself as she brushed them away. In a week or two, everything would get back to normal.

And Simon would just be the neighbor she waved to when she came and went from the house.

Her heart sank at the thought.

Chapter Four

Standing at the back door, Risa noticed the gathering black clouds in the early evening sky and frowned. A few days ago a line of thunderstorms had passed through and turned into a tornado watch. Thank goodness none had formed. Although Janetta had shown her the storm cellar, they hadn't had to use it throughout the spring when tornadoes were the most common. The house didn't have a full basement, yet an outside entrance led to the cellar that could be used in an emergency. Risa didn't want to think about being closed in there in the damp and dark. Still, if it meant relative safety until a dangerous storm blew over, she'd take Francie and retreat there if she had to.

Now she was more worried about the clothes she had hanging on the line. Janetta's drier was on the blink, and the repairman was supposed to come first thing tomorrow morning. Risa did two batches of laundry each day for Francie. She couldn't believe it was nearly the end of July and her daughter was already ten days old. She couldn't imagine *not* having her around now.

Although she'd been busy with Francie, snatching sleep when she could, she couldn't help thinking about Simon. She hadn't really seen him since the day he'd kissed her. On Saturday night he'd had some friends over and she could hear them talking and laughing on the patio. But she'd stayed inside.

She knew he was home now. His sheriff's SUV was parked out front and the lights were on in his kitchen. He was probably eating dinner in front of the TV and following the course of the storm...or the nightly news.

Gusts of wind suddenly buffeted the house, rattling the door. A few moments later, raindrops pinged on the windows. Optimistically, Risa had hoped the storm would blow over. Now she knew she had to gather the clothes from the line. With a glance at Francie, who was sleeping in the bassinet in the living room, she ran outside. The wind had wrapped the baby blankets and a few towels around the line. Terry playsuits and sheets pulled against the clothespins as the wind strove to grab them away.

Picking up the small wicker laundry basket, Risa ran to the end of the line just as the rain's patter became a downpour. While she untangled the first sheet, she got drenched. Yanking it free, she tossed it into the wash basket. As she fumbled with the clothespins on a terry playsuit, Simon strode up beside her. "Why not just leave them?" he asked.

"Because they're just washed and I need some of

them to dry. Janetta's drier isn't working. But you don't have to get wet, too."

Still dressed in his uniform, he ignored her remarks and quickly detached clothespins from material, tossing everything into the wash basket. Hefting it into his arm, he moved down the line quickly with her until they'd gathered all the clothes. Then they ran to the back porch and into the kitchen.

They were both dripping.

Risa grabbed a few dishtowels from the drawer and handed two of them to Simon. As she mopped her face, she knew the rest was hopeless. Her hair stuck to her cheek, her knit top molded to her breasts, and her shorts clung to her thighs.

Simon's quick glance at her as he toweled his hair took it all in. "What's wrong with Janetta's drier?"

"I'm not sure. I think the heating unit went out. The repairman's coming tomorrow."

He tossed his towel onto the counter. "There's no point in drying off, since I have to go back out there. I'll take the basket with me and dry the clothes over at my place. I'll bring them back later."

She was about to towel her hair, but now she faced him instead. After not seeing or talking to him for days, he thought he knew what was best for her. "Do you *always* have to take charge?"

His gaze went from her wet clothes to her eyes. Instead of taking offense, he answered matter-of-factly, "Yep. It's second nature."

"Why?"

"I grew up having to take charge. My mother went

to pieces when my dad went to prison. I watched for the bills and made sure they got paid. If I wanted to eat, I cooked. When I went to stay with my aunt, who was a lot older than my mother, I kept doing the same things I had done at home. Besides…taking charge comes in handy when you're a sheriff," he added with a smile.

Todd had tried to take charge of every situation, too. The thing was, Todd's way and Simon's way seemed different somehow. She just hadn't figured out how, yet.

"So what about the clothes?" he asked motioning to the wash basket. "Do you want them dry, or do you want them wet?"

Simon was one of the most practical men she'd ever known, and she had to smile at his cut-to-the-chase question. "I'd much rather have them dry. Did you eat supper yet?"

"No. I was going to order a pizza."

"I have a roast in the crockpot. I was going to make rice and have some vegetables. I have to eat fairly plain because of breast-feeding Francie. But I have plenty. I can have it all ready by the time the clothes come out of the drier."

When Simon crossed to her and stood before her, she inhaled his musky scent mixed with rain. She shivered and it had nothing to do with being wet. As he wiped a drop of rain rolling along her cheek, she could feel herself opening up to him, could feel herself accepting his help without resentment or question. Her insides quivered, and she remembered every moment of their kiss.

"You're bound and determined to repay me for everything I do for you, aren't you?" he asked.

Finding her voice, she murmured, "I don't like to be in debt to anyone."

Simon's gaze went to her lips, then dropped lower to her breasts. Then he let out a pent-up breath. "You'd better change."

She felt her nipples becoming hard, and she couldn't believe his mere attention could arouse her like this.

Suddenly Simon moved to the table to pick up the laundry basket and went to the door.

After Risa took a deep breath, she realized in a way she was relieved by his departure. Yet in another way and totally illogically, she missed his presence.

Reestablishing her equilibrium, she felt as if she should do something a little special since Simon was coming to supper. After she changed clothes, she took a box of strawberries from the refrigerator. Then she washed and sliced them to spoon them over vanilla ice cream for dessert.

She'd just set the berries aside, put vegetables on the stove to steam and placed the bowl of rice on the counter, when Francie awakened. Turning the stove to low, she went to the living room to tend to her daughter.

Although Risa cooed and made baby sounds at Francie, her daughter didn't quiet until she was changed and suckling at her mom's breast. Risa sat in the peach-and-yellow recliner-rocker, looking down at Francie as she nursed. She was totally engrossed in her, awash in the tender, motherly feelings that always overwhelmed her when she breast-fed, marveling all over again at Francie's perfect little ear, when she heard a noise and looked up.

Simon had changed from his uniform into a black polo shirt and blue jeans. He was wearing sneakers now instead of boots. That's probably why she hadn't heard him come in. The expression on his face when he saw Francie feeding at Risa's exposed breast sent shivers up Risa's spine. The look in his eyes urged her to remember the way his lips had felt on hers, the glide of his tongue into her mouth, the racing of her pulse.

But the next moment, a dark flush stained his cheeks and he said in a low rumble, "I'll wait for you in the kitchen."

He turned away as if he were watching something too private to witness.

After Francie finished nursing, Risa put her in a baby carrier and took it out to the kitchen. As she set it on the table, she glanced at Simon. He was taking rice from the microwave. She'd been surprised by his reaction. After all, he was a man of the world, she was sure. According to rumors, he'd seen his share of bare breasts.

Gathering two plates and two glasses from the cupboard, Risa placed them on the table. "Thanks for making the rice."

"No problem." An awkward silence dropped between them. After a short pause, he closed the door to the microwave. "I didn't mean to barge in on you like that."

"That's okay. I'm going to have to get used to feeding Francie…with other people around."

"You're going to do it in public?"

"I'll always try to be discreet. In class I learned how to use a blanket to cover everything."

He leaned against the counter and studied her. "Good. Because I felt like I'd stepped into sacred territory when I came into that room and saw you."

"It's just going to be a natural part of me being a mother."

"It turned me on," he stated bluntly.

Her pulse raced faster, and she wasn't sure what to say to that. Suddenly she realized he was frowning because he might be thinking about other men watching her, too.

"I...see," she said quietly.

Stepping around the kitchen chair, he stood before her. When he did, she caught a whiff of masculine soap. He must have showered.

"Breast-feeding might feel natural to you," he warned, "but you're a damn beautiful woman, Risa. When I saw you in there, it was hard for me to remember you're still grieving over your husband."

"Simon..." She didn't know how to put into words what she'd felt about Todd's death. "My marriage—" She paused. "It wasn't perfect." That was an understatement if ever she'd made one.

"You had problems?" he asked as if it was important for him to know.

Reminding herself she'd only really known Simon for three weeks, reminding herself that he was a take-charge man and that she never wanted a man telling her what to do again, she murmured, "I'd rather not talk about my marriage." She was still sorting out what had happened…what she could have done differently.

"Because it's painful?" he prodded.

"Because it's private."

Cocking his head, he reached out and his thumb gently stroked her cheek. "I can respect that, but keeping everything all bottled up inside of you isn't going to help you get over it, either."

"I'm getting over it," she assured him and moved toward her daughter. Francie had become her life, and she was all that mattered now.

"The past has a way of intruding in the present." He sounded as if his had done that more than once.

She knew he was right, but she couldn't share hers with him and didn't know if she'd ever be able to. Sharing required trust, and trusting a man just didn't seem to be within her realm of possibility. "I'm going to concentrate on Francie."

"What about *your* needs?" Simon asked as if he knew what they might be.

"Mothers put aside their needs for their children, and that's what I'm going to do. I'm going to build a life for the two of us." She didn't add the words "without a man" but the message was clear.

"That's what a *good* mother does—sacrifices for her kids," Simon concluded as he moved to the crockpot where the roast was cooking, and the tension between them broke. "I can see you're going to be a terrific mom, Risa. I admire that."

She remembered then what he'd told her about his mother, and she wished she hadn't said what she had.

But as if none of it affected him, he lifted the glass lid. "I'll carve this for you. Just give me something to put it on."

He was taking charge again, but Risa found she didn't mind. That thought was as unsettling as his presence in her kitchen. Maybe by the time they finished supper, the electricity she felt whenever she got near him would diminish. She hoped so because she really did intend to concentrate on her life and Francie's…without a man.

Simon drove back to Cedar Corners from a meeting in Oklahoma City the following afternoon. He thought about his supper last night with Risa, about the feelings he didn't know what to do with, about the wariness in her eyes that told him she didn't trust him on some level. He wanted the whole story about her marriage, but good sense told him to stay out of it. Good sense told him to stay away from *her*. Good sense told him she was an independent woman who could manage just fine on her own.

Yet his good sense had a hard time battling against the pictures of Francie's delivery, his awe at holding her in his arms, the smile on Risa's face when he'd handed her her baby, their kiss that had reinvented his idea of what a kiss should be.

On the outskirts of Cedar Corners, Simon scanned the farmland, looking for anything out of place in his territory. It wasn't much of a distraction, but if he could just get Risa out of his head…

The old grain storage silo on the Conniff place

caught his eye, and he wondered if any of the deputies had checked on the abandoned farmhouse lately. It was one of those unofficial assignments. Any deputy in the area knew to check it out to make sure teenagers hadn't broken in again or vagrants weren't having a picnic that might destroy the place. The Conniff family hadn't been able to pay the taxes on it or make a living, and they'd moved out of state with relatives over two years ago. It had been for sale that long. Their insurance company had boarded it up after a year.

Windows being boarded up were an invitation to some kinds of folks. Simon kept his town as clean of crime and the temptations of crime as he could. Now if he could just catch the vandals who were eluding everyone in the sheriff's office...

He shook his head. Probably teenagers with too much time on their hands. He hoped that's all it was.

The lane to the Conniff farm was almost overgrown with weeds, but stones still crunched under his tires as he drove toward the house, thinking this was a great property if someone just put some work into it. It could be subdivided and acreage could be sold off for a housing development. They could plot off nice big lots with room for kids to play.

Since when had he started thinking about kids and the yards they had to play in?

Through the tall weeds swaying in the wind, he caught sight of the front of the house with its wraparound porch. Suddenly he went on alert. Something was off. Something was wrong. His instincts had always been good, and he trusted them now.

He immediately realized what had alerted him. The old screen door on the front porch that had been precariously near falling off its hinges had done just that. But it hadn't fallen to the porch floor. It was propped up.

The storm wouldn't have done that. It would have taken it down.

Deciding to let caution lead him, he pulled over into the weeds, cut his engine, and leaned toward the locked glove compartment where he kept his gun. Removing his Glock from the compartment, he tucked it into the waistband of his trousers. He then opened his door, stepping out into the weeds, and closed it quietly.

There probably wasn't any cause for concern. Maybe some kids had been snooping around. However, in his mind, he went over bulletins he'd gotten on the computer—the be-on-the-lookout messages and flyers that had come into the office about crimes in the area, missing kids, outstanding warrants.

Brambles scratched his arms as he crouched then moved through the weeds until he rounded the back of the house where the lane ended. His heart began pumping as he saw two cars—a Toyota with patches of rust that looked about ten years old, and a battered pickup that didn't look much better. Memorizing the license plates, he returned to his SUV and called them in.

Five very long minutes later, he got the information he needed. The pickup had been used in a bank robbery in Cushing two days ago. Son of a gun! If the bank robbers had been holed up in his jurisdiction for two days…

Calling for backup, he headed for the rear entrance of the house. These guys would be in jail by nightfall if he had anything to say about it.

Risa had flipped on the TV before she'd settled on the sofa to feed Francie. Between laundry, visits from her mother and Lucy, and Francie's feedings, the day had seemed to speed by. Now she cuddled her daughter to her breast and was surprised to see a long view of Cedar Corners on the Oklahoma City news. Then she was even more surprised to see a picture of Simon flash on the screen.

A news anchor was standing in front of the old Conniff farmhouse at the edge of Cedar Corners. Risa's heart started beating faster as the anchor proclaimed, "Sheriff Simon Blackstone of Cedar Corners is a hero tonight. He'd been returning from a meeting in Oklahoma City when, dedicated lawman that he is, he checked on the old Conniff place on the outskirts of town. There he found bank robbers who had stolen money from a branch bank of Keystone National in Cushing two days ago. They attempted to leave before Sheriff Blackstone's backup arrived. Single-handedly, he took both men into custody where they are now awaiting transfer in the Cedar Corners jail. There will be a press conference in the cafeteria of the elementary school at seven-thirty this evening. Needless to say, this is more excitement than Cedar Corners has seen in a decade. And Sheriff Simon Blackstone is at the center of it."

Risa found herself asking Francie, "The reporter

would have said something if Simon had been hurt, right?"

She could call Simon later, but she didn't want to bother him. She also didn't particularly want him to know she was concerned about him.

The elementary school was only two blocks away. She couldn't drive yet, but she could easily walk there with Francie in her papoose pouch. Hopefully, she could slip into the press conference unnoticed and find out exactly what had happened…if Simon was unharmed. It would give her a chance to stretch her legs and get some exercise. Francie would get some fresh air and the whole excursion might put Risa's mind to rest so she could sleep tonight.

When Risa entered the lobby of the elementary school, people filed into the cafeteria. There were news vans and cable wires, suited men and what seemed like half the population of Cedar Corners in shorts and T-shirts. She saw people she knew, parents of students she'd taught, two of the elementary-school teachers. All wanted a glimpse of Francie. She proudly showed off her daughter, all the while thinking about Simon and what had happened this afternoon.

There were no vacant seats, but a tall man in jeans and a Stetson saw Risa and her baby and offered her his chair. Thanking him, she slipped into it, not wanting Simon to notice her in the crowd. She spotted him as soon as he entered the cafeteria from the kitchen entrance up front. There were two tables set up there, several chairs and a standup microphone. Reporters lined the first row the entire width of the cafeteria. She could tell who they were from the tape recorders, notebooks, and camcorders. She wouldn't want to be the one standing in front of them.

The school was air-conditioned, and large ceiling fans overhead stirred the air that was getting warmer in the crowded cafeteria.

Simon was dressed in uniform tonight, though he'd taken off his Stetson and laid it on the serving counter behind the table. She noticed a bandage on one of his arms and scratches on his forearms. He looked tired, and she imagined it had already been a day and a half for him.

The mayor, a short, balding man in his late fifties, came to the microphone first. Jim Gallagher was well liked because he kept the budget in the black and the stoplights working. Now as he stood before everyone, the crowd quieted.

"I just wanted to welcome you all here. I know you're interested in what happened today, and you don't want to hear it from me. You want to hear it from the man who's responsible for putting two bank robbers behind bars. If you don't already know him, let me present Sheriff Simon Blackstone to you."

As Simon walked to the mike, the crowd applauded. He looked mighty uncomfortable as they kept applauding, and Risa could tell he didn't like being in the limelight. After a forced smile, he held up his hands for everyone to quiet.

As soon as they were silent, he began with, "I'm going to explain what happened today, then I'll take a few questions."

In succinct sentences he told the same story the news anchor had related on TV, except he downplayed his part in it.

When he finished, a brunette in the first row stood up and asked, "Is it true you arrested both men single-handedly?"

"They came out the back door before backup arrived," he replied.

"Did you have to shoot at them?" she asked, following up quickly.

"I pulled my gun. No shots were fired."

A reporter on the other side of the room shouted, "I heard one guy tried to take off and you had to tackle him. He told one of the deputies he tried to knife you but you used some kind of martial arts on him."

Simon looked even more uncomfortable. "Actually I tripped him. Before he could get to his feet, I handcuffed him."

After Simon took a few more questions, Risa decided he was definitely understating what had happened that afternoon and his part in it.

Finally he ended with, "I want to thank Deputies Foster and Garrity for their immediate response to my backup call and their expertise in handling the arrangements for our suspects' transit and transfer. Now I'll turn this back over to the mayor."

The press conference would have wound down with that, but there was one reporter determined not to let Simon go. He had a cameraman with him and the tape was rolling.

As Simon stepped away from the microphone, the

suited man called, "Your father died in prison. Did you think about that when you pulled your weapon today?"

There had been rustle and movement and chattering before the question. Now heavy silence fell over the cafeteria.

A dark flush stained Simon's face but that was the only indication of his anger. His voice was calm but it had a sharp edge as he stared down the reporter, then answered, "My personal background gave me the motivation to become a law enforcement officer. But it has nothing to do with how I do my job. I'm sworn to uphold the law, and that's what I do."

Simon walked away.

Risa remembered how defiantly he'd told her about his childhood. Had even a quarter of the citizens of Cedar Corners known about his background before now? That particular information hadn't floated around during the pre-election campaign.

What was Simon thinking...feeling?

From hero to a convict's son in a matter of seconds.

Not hesitating, Risa stood, made her way up the side aisle of the cafeteria and left through the side door. Francie was asleep close to her chest, and she kept her arms around her baby as she walked.

Spotting Simon's quick long stride as he headed toward his SUV in the parking lot, she hurried, still holding Francie close. When he was about to get into his car, she called, "Simon. Wait."

He did but didn't look happy about it. When she was standing by his car door, he studied her, holding the door loosely with one hand. "What were you doing in there?"

"I came because…"

"Because you were curious like everyone else," he filled in with a shake of his head. "Did you find out what you wanted to know?"

"I didn't want to know anything except that you were all right." She could see the scratches on his arms up close now and the bandage. "You *are* all right, aren't you?"

Something deep and dark flickered in his eyes. "I'm perfectly fine." His expression softened a bit as he rubbed the back of his neck. "It's been a long day, and I still have paperwork to do. I'm headed back to the office. How did you get here?"

"I walked." When frown lines creased his forehead, she added, "It wasn't that far. I do need to start exercising again. Walking is a good way to get back into it."

"Do you want a ride home? I can swing by there."

Simon Blackstone had gone out of his way for her too many times in the past few weeks. She wasn't going to use him as a taxi service, too. "No. As I said, I want to walk." She patted Francie's back. "She'll probably sleep the whole way home."

He peered up at the dusky sky. "You should make it before dark."

"Simon, about what happened in there…"

"I don't want to talk about it."

"If it's on the news tonight—"

"It doesn't matter," he said cutting her off. "I'm surprised somebody didn't dig it up during the election. If the people who voted for me are going to hold my background against me, then I guess I'll move on after the next election."

He opened his door wider. "If you really don't want a ride, I've got to get going."

He'd gone remote on her. His attitude annoyed her but it didn't scare her. It was so different from Todd's when he'd gotten angry.

She shouldn't be making comparisons between the two men.

"I hope you have a quieter day tomorrow," she said sincerely then turned and walked away from Simon, knowing she was beginning to care much too much about what he said and what he did.

She was going to put a stop to that tonight.

Chapter Five

When Simon left the sheriff's office, his head was pounding and a curl of guilt gnawed in his chest. He had been more brusque with Risa than he should have been. He only had one excuse. The day had taken its toll, and the question about his father had poured too much salt on an old wound.

He saw lights in Risa's upstairs and downstairs as he pulled into his garage in the back and made his way up to his patio. The night was quiet, and he probably wouldn't have noticed her in her yard if she hadn't been wearing white…if the moon hadn't been so high and full…if the stillness hadn't been so absolute that he could hear the soft rustle of movement in the grass only twenty feet away.

The low boxwood hedge concealed little as he crossed to the edge of it, and in spite of himself took the path into her backyard.

She was unaware of him as she stood barefoot in the grass, looking up to the heavens. Although she was wearing a long white T-shirt that skimmed her knees, in the shadows he couldn't tell if she had clothes under it or not. He should leave her the hell alone. He should go take a cold shower and get some sleep.

But her profile drove him forward. She was in another world, totally engrossed in it. And the purity of her standing there so still, her cameo face tipped to the moon, her long wavy hair brushing her shoulders in the breeze, socked him in the gut.

"Risa?" he called softly, not wanting to startle her.

A small gasp escaped her lips that told him he had startled her anyway. But when she saw him, she smiled. "Just getting home?" she asked.

As he took a few steps closer, he could see she was wearing a bra and panties under the thin nightshirt. Somehow their shadows were even more seductive than her nakedness would have been.

He cleared his throat. "Yeah. More paperwork than I knew what to do with."

"And now you just want a good night's sleep."

"That's about it."

"Are you going to be able to fall asleep? It must all still be on your mind."

It definitely was and he really didn't want to talk about it. Besides, the idea of falling asleep was creating visions of Risa beside him in his bed…under him in his bed.

"What are you doing out here?" he asked gruffly.

"I just needed to wiggle my toes in the grass, breathe

in some un-air-conditioned air and look at the sky for a while. I haven't done any of those things since before Francie was born."

"I guess kids can take up all twenty-four hours in the day."

"I guess anything you love can."

"I wouldn't know about that," he muttered. He'd never really loved anything that much, or anyone—not even Renée. She hadn't taken up that much time. He'd relegated her to date nights, phone calls, bits of time in their busy schedules.

"Do you still *not* want to talk about the press conference?" Risa asked softly.

He blew out a breath because she could read him too well. "There's no point."

"There is if the reporter's question causes a backlash in the next election. Are you worried about that?"

"I said what I had to say on the subject. If my father's notoriety keeps people in Cedar Corners from voting for me, then maybe I *shouldn't* be sheriff for another term."

When she took a step closer, the moonlight caught red strands in her hair, turning them to fire. "I think most of them will look at what you've accomplished so far. Children shouldn't be judged by their parents' actions."

Jamming his hand in his pocket so he didn't reach out and touch her, he replied, "They shouldn't, but they are. I always have been. From the teachers in school expecting me to turn out like my father, to the neighbors who loved to gossip about our family. When my mom took off, I couldn't get away from the pitying stares and neighbors gossiping that I was better off."

"You heard all that?"

"Gossip gets around. Somehow adults think kids can't hear. I'd be standing in the neighborhood convenience store and somebody would see me and make a comment to someone they were with. I got used to it. Somehow I thought as an adult I could shuck it all off."

"Have you?" Her voice was suddenly curious.

A stiffer breeze came from somewhere beyond the trees and brought the scent of her lotion or soap to him. It was as sweet as honeysuckle and as potent as brandy. Suddenly he wanted to know if his background made a difference to *her*.

"After I became sheriff here, I thought I'd left everything behind in Oklahoma City. But your past follows you around and sometimes you have to step back into it. I was dating a woman. I thought we could have a future. The thing is—I don't believe two people can have a future without honesty. I told her about my parents...my father's background...about living with my aunt. At the time she acted as if it was no big deal. She was a good actress. Because after that night, when I called her, she didn't pick up and she didn't return my calls. I got the message real quick."

"Simon, I'm sorry."

"I didn't tell you so you'd feel sorry," he said in a gravelly voice.

"Why did you tell me?"

Maybe she didn't mean the question as an invitation...but it was. He took a few steps closer to her and just breathed in everything about her for a few seconds. "I told you because I wanted to see if it mattered to *you*. I figure after what we've been through, we should stay honest."

"Because we're becoming good friends?" Her voice was so soft it was like a caress.

"I'm not sure."

Then he was gazing into her dark brown eyes, seeing the moon's shine reflected in them. He was taking that extra little step closer, this time hoping beyond hope she wouldn't move away. He was remembering everything about who his parents had been and who he was, for some insane reason hoping Risa could accept it all.

Simon considered himself an expert kisser. He'd been doing it long enough to master it. But when he kissed Risa… The last time he'd felt as if he were kissing a girl for the first time, and tonight—

She was so damn soft and sweet and sensual, though he didn't know if she even knew how seductive her vulnerability could be. When his lips brushed hers, he felt as if someone had set his body on fire. This time when he kissed her, he took her lips the way he'd wanted to take them for months. Her little moan of pleasure urged him to bring her closer, slide his hands into her hair, immediately put more depth into the kiss. His tongue plumbed the corners of her mouth and then suddenly she was giving back, she was tasting him, too, arching her breasts against his chest, kneading his shoulders with her hands. He noticed something about this kiss he'd never noticed with a woman before—it was so damn intimate that he almost felt as if he were making

love with her. Almost. The visions in his head had
played over and over in his dreams.

Although his body was shouting at him to finish
this, he knew reality from a dream. He knew Risa
wasn't the type of woman to be satisfied with one
night...he understood she'd just had a baby and sex was
out of the question.

Breaking the kiss, he pulled back, dropped his arms,
then tipped down his Stetson so she couldn't see what
was going on on his face. "You'd better go in." It came
out like a growl.

Her dazed look cleared and she nodded. "I guess I'd
better." But before she turned away from him, she
added, "Simon, you were a hero today. I won't forget
that, and I don't think anyone else will, either."

Then she went up the porch steps and disappeared
inside.

When he heard the click of the lock, he started toward his house, thinking about what she'd said and
hoping it was true.

In spite of her good sense warning Risa to stay away
from Simon, she was disappointed she hadn't seen him
over the weekend. He'd been gone all day Saturday.
She'd spent Sunday at her mom's, and Simon's house
had been dark when Lucy had dropped her off at
Janetta's that night.

When Risa thought about everything Simon had
done for her in the past few weeks, she felt indebted.
Actually she felt *more* than indebted. His kisses took
her on a sensual journey she'd never expected to go on.

She'd never felt sensations like she experienced with Simon when he kissed her. She'd never expected to want to *be* with a man again. Not after the way Todd had treated her—like a possession. But as she told herself once more that Simon *wasn't* Todd, she found herself wanting to spend more time with him.

She knew any thank-you she came up with had to be low-key or he wouldn't accept it. She still couldn't drive but that didn't have to be an impediment in a town the size of Cedar Corners. Walking was good exercise and she could do it with Francie. Doubting that anyone ever brought Simon homemade treats, early Monday morning she baked a pan of sticky buns. She'd use the new stroller her sister had given her as a baby present, and Francie could sleep under its shaded canopy on the way to the sheriff's office. Risa had a soft-sided carrier in which she put the sticky buns and two cans of orange juice. It fit on the back of the stroller. After she dropped off the snack for Simon, she'd take Francie to her pediatrician's appointment. It was a good plan, and Risa hoped Simon would think so, too.

The early August morning was already warm, and a breeze was blowing as Risa took her time pushing the stroller. She'd worn a bright yellow sundress with straps trimmed with daisies. Her white sandals were comfortable and with a straw hat perched on her head to shade her from the sun, she enjoyed the walk.

The sheriff's office was only three blocks from Janetta's house. As Risa approached the one-story brick building, she wondered if she should have called. But if she'd called, her treat wouldn't have been a surprise.

A deputy was exiting the building as she approached it and he held the door for her. She thanked him and pushed the stroller over the threshold's bump. As soon as she stepped inside, she considered the fact that she might have made a monumental mistake. Every eye in the place was on her from the receptionist to the dispatcher to two deputies standing in an area with four desks and computers.

The receptionist scanned Risa first and then the stroller. "Can I help you?"

"I hope so," Risa returned politely. "I'm here to see Sheriff Blackstone."

The receptionist, a blond, frizzy-haired woman with huge hoop earrings, exchanged a look with the dispatcher—a middle-aged woman with gray hair who looked like somebody's favorite aunt.

"What's your business with the sheriff?" the receptionist asked.

That surprised Risa, but she supposed they couldn't bother Simon with details that weren't important. She wasn't quite sure sticky buns were important. "Could you just tell him Risa Parker is here? I...brought a snack." There was no reason to hide why she'd come. Maybe.

After another long look at Risa's straw hat and Francie sleeping in the stroller, the blonde pushed a button on the console on her desk. "Sheriff Blackstone?" she asked sweetly.

"Yes, Myra." His deep voice sounded sexy even over the intercom, Risa thought, beginning to get a bit nervous.

"You have company. A Risa Parker."

A few silent moments ticked by. "I'll be right out."

One of the deputies had taken a seat at his desk, though the other waited as if he expected a show to start soon.

A few minutes later, Simon emerged from a doorway behind the receptionist's desk. Risa suspected it was a hall that led to his office, interview rooms and the small jail where the bank robbers had been imprisoned for a few hours before their transfer.

When Simon saw her, he didn't smile. But his eyes lit with those sparks she always glimpsed before he kissed her.

"This is a surprise," he said as he crossed to her.

"Maybe this was truly a bad idea," she acknowledged in a low voice. "But you've done so many nice things for us lately, I brought you sticky buns. If you're too busy, I can just leave them."

He clasped her arm as if she might do that. "No, I'm not too busy and I deserve a break like anyone else. I just never take it."

The deputy who was still standing grinned. "We shove fast food at him at regular intervals so he doesn't starve."

Simon rolled his eyes. "Risa Parker, meet Anson Foster." He motioned to the deputy sitting at the desk. "And that's Dave Garrity."

"I know who she is now," the receptionist said with a sly smile. "This is the baby you delivered."

Simon pointed to his receptionist. "That's Myra and our dispatcher's name is Nancy. None of them believed the rumor that I helped Francie come into this world."

"Juiciest rumor running around *this* town in a long time," Myra said with a nod of her head.

"Do you want to come back to my office?" Simon asked Risa, ignoring Myra's comment. "It's nice and cool there."

Feeling a little less uncomfortable now, Risa asked, "Are you sure you have time?"

"Positively sure. Come on."

But as Simon took hold of Francie's stroller and pushed it past the receptionist's desk, she heard Anson say to Dave, "He's never taken one of his women back *there* before."

Risa knew Simon heard it, too, but pretended he didn't as he led her down the hallway to the first door on the right. Was she wrong to come here? She'd heard Simon played the field, never dating one woman very long. Yet he told her he'd tried to get involved once. Did that mean deep down he wanted a serious relationship?

Did *she?* Is that why she was here?

No. She was here to thank Simon. That was all.

"You have a friendly staff," she said lightly as she entered his office and saw how organized it was. But then that didn't surprise her. Simon struck her as the efficient type.

After he parked Francie's stroller under the window, he began clearing his desk. "They're great, but sometimes they're too nosy."

Risa took off her hat and laid it on a spare chair, then raised the canopy on the stroller so she could see Francie from wherever she sat. Her daughter was sleeping peacefully, and Risa gently touched her cheek.

Simon had been stacking file folders but when she looked up, she found him watching her. Deciding since they had always been honest with each other, she asked, "Is it true you never brought a woman back here before?"

"Other than any I might have arrested?" he asked with a sly smile.

"I won't ask about those," she decided in keeping with his light tone.

Taking the stack of folders to the bookshelves, he found an empty spot and deposited them there.

After Risa took the carrier from the back of Francie's stroller, Simon was beside her in a minute taking it from her hands.

"It's not heavy."

His hand had covered hers on the handle, and he looked at her now with the heat that brought back explicit memories of their kisses.

After he looked in the carrier and saw the wrapped sticky buns and the orange juice, he said, "Did you bake these?"

She just nodded.

"You didn't have to go to all that trouble."

"It wasn't any trouble. I like to bake."

The way his gaze studied her, she felt as if he was looking right through her, seeing places she'd rather keep hidden.

Finally he broke eye contact and as he glanced at the sleeping baby, a serious expression came over Simon's face.

Risa sat in the chair across the desk from him. While

he unwrapped the sticky buns, she took out the paper plates and plastic forks she'd also put in the carrier.

"I never *have* brought a woman back here, Risa."

Her gaze shot to his and she waited.

"I always thought it was better to keep my work separated from my personal life."

She felt terrifically uncomfortable. "And I made a scene with the stroller and the carrier—"

Immediately he shook his head. "No, you didn't make a scene. The thing is—I don't mind your being here. In fact..." He motioned to everything on his desk, "This is nice."

His words gave her a warm glow inside.

Right after he ate a few bites of the pastry, he took a swig from the can of orange juice and then sat back in his chair. "I've never been friends with a woman before." After a pause he added, "But I think I've told you a lot more about my life than you've told me about yours."

She played with a pecan with her fork. "That's not so. You've been to my mother's house. You've seen my whole family except for Janetta. She'll be home in a week, by the way."

"Will she?" He studied the remainder of the bun on his plate, then must have decided to go after what he wanted. "I know a little bit about your family, but I don't know anything about your marriage."

A chill skipped up Risa's spine. Simon seemed to be asking her to confide in him. Yet telling him about Todd was so much more complicated than that. He'd see how weak she had been. He'd see how foolhardy she'd been to think time and her love could convince Todd to act differently. He might even blame her for Todd's accident as she sometimes did herself. And most of all, if she told him about all of it, she'd have to trust him.

"Risa?"

"What?"

"Why can't you tell me about your marriage?"

"I don't feel comfortable discussing it. It's private. Marriages should be."

"That's not it," Simon said with certainty.

"Do you think I'm lying to you?"

He considered her for a very long moment. "No, you're evading me. I want to know why."

"We don't know each other that well, Simon."

"If you mean we don't have a long history, well, we don't. But I caught your daughter in my hands when she was born. I've spent time with your family and our kisses have kept me awake at night. I don't know everything there is to know about you, and that's why I'm asking you about your marriage."

Now she was sorry she'd come. She wasn't ready for this. How foolish she had been. Repercussions from her marriage and Todd's death weren't something she could just shove aside because she wanted to get on with her life. Telling Simon about it couldn't help. In fact, it might make everything that much worse.

She suddenly felt very tired. The walk had played her out and this conversation had added to it. Obviously she wasn't recovered yet. "I don't want to talk about my marriage," she said in a low voice.

"So much for being friends." He sounded a bit angry.

Still she found she wasn't afraid of Simon's anger as she had been of Todd's. Simon's was clear and clean, coming from the situation in front of them.

"Maybe you need to be a *patient* friend," she suggested.

Francie began to stir, making little whimpering noises. Simon glanced at her and then back at Risa. "I've been told I *am* a patient man. I just never had to use that patience with a woman before."

"They always give you what you want, when you want it?"

He laughed. "You know how to get to the heart of the matter, don't you?"

"You have a reputation, Simon." As much as he wanted to know about her marriage, she wanted to know about that.

"Most of it is earned, I suppose," he admitted wryly. "I tried something serious with Renée. It didn't work. I just never imagined sticking with one woman would be in the cards for me. As far as ever having kids...I had no role model. I don't even know what a family should be."

He was wrong about that. She'd seen him interact with her family. She'd seen him with Francie. Simon could easily learn how to be a family man, but did he want to be? "I guess you could remain a bachelor all your life. Some men do."

"A bachelor and sheriff, concentrating on poker games with my buddies? That could be a life." His tone was sardonic and she wasn't sure how he really felt about it.

Francie's whimpering turned to small cries. Risa

pushed her chair back and went to her daughter, lifting her out of the stroller. "I'm going to have to feed her."

Simon noticed that her dress buttoned down the front. "I'll leave while you do."

He hadn't finished his snack and she didn't want to put him out of his own office. Taking the blanket from the bottom of the stroller that she could use to cover herself while Francie nursed, she suggested, "You finish eating. Isn't there another room I could use?"

He thought about it. "Only the interview rooms."

"Do you think Francie will pick up bad vibes?" she joked.

With a shake of his head, he laughed. "No, I guess not. They're just pretty barren. When I think about you feeding Francie—" He stopped. They both knew where that would take him.

"Come on, I'll put you in room #1. But I want you to lock the door."

She raised curious eyes to his.

"I don't want someone walking in on you, and that could happen."

A half hour later, after Francie nursed, Risa returned with her to Simon's office. He was at his computer keyboard.

As soon as he saw her, he motioned to her plate still sitting on the desk. "You go ahead and eat."

Risa had changed Francie in the interview room, too, and now she packed the diaper bag on the back of the stroller. "I'm not really hungry, and we have to be going. Not only so you can work, but I have to take Francie to the pediatrician."

Suddenly something occurred to Simon. "How did you get here?"

"We walked. It's not very far."

"And where's the doctor's office?" he asked.

"Two blocks over—on Chestnut."

"And that will be another four blocks back to your house. You had a baby two weeks ago."

"Walking is good for me." She'd probably planned a bigger excursion than she should handle.

"Maybe so, but overdoing it isn't. I'll drive you to your appointment."

"Simon, you have a job here."

"Don't I know it," he mumbled. "But I was stuck in this office most of the weekend. I deserve some comp time."

"You want to use it taking me to a doctor's appointment?"

"Sure, why not? I can catch up on all my favorite magazines in the office."

"You don't have to wait, you know."

Simon pressed a button on the keyboard, then stood. "Be honest with me about something, Risa."

"What?"

"Do you want me to take you to the doctor's or would you prefer to go yourself?"

Chapter Six

From the piercing look in Simon's eyes, Risa knew he wanted the truth from her. And she wanted the truth from him. "It would be great if you'd drive me to the doctor's and take me home. But...I don't want you doing it out of some sense of duty."

He took his Stetson from a hat peg on the wall and plunked it onto his head. "It's more than duty. The kiss between us the other night had nothing to do with duty. There's fire between us, Risa, and maybe we're going to get burned, but it's too hot to ignore and I'd like to find out what it's all about."

"I don't know if I'm ready for any of it," she said quietly.

"That's fair. Why don't we just take this one step at a time and see where it gets us?"

The suggestion sounded so simple, yet she knew it

wasn't. After ten steps into this, she could get hurt, and so could he. Yet if she didn't try, she'd be letting her marriage to Todd and everything that happened in it control her. She couldn't let her marriage to Todd shadow the rest of her life. She'd have to show Simon that she wasn't afraid to take a risk.

"One step at a time," she agreed.

A half hour later, Simon had borrowed a car seat from one of his deputies and anchored it in the back of the Sheriff's SUV. After Risa showed him how the stroller collapsed, Simon drove her and Francie to their appointment. He'd seen the looks Anson and Dave had thrown at each other, the knowing smiles between Myra and Nancy. Maybe he'd be the butt of gossip for a day or so, but it just didn't matter right now. He felt a bond with Risa he'd never felt with another woman. Maybe it was because of her daughter...maybe it wasn't.

After they'd arrived at the old house turned into a pediatrics clinic, Simon helped Risa out and unhitched Francie from the back. He was getting more sure of picking her up now, and it seemed as if she'd grown already.

"Want me to carry her inside?" he asked.

"You can if you'd like."

He found that he'd like that very much.

In the waiting room, Risa went to the receptionist's window while Simon settled in a chair with Francie. He heard the receptionist tell Risa, "Dr. Gracy had an emergency and is tied up at the hospital, but Dr. Winslow will see Francie today if that's all right with you."

After Risa came to sit beside him, he studied her. "Do you know Dr. Winslow?"

"I've never met him, but I studied his credentials before I chose this pediatrics practice to take care of Francie. Most group practices rotate doctors now anyway. It will be good for me to meet him."

Risa had taken to parenthood so easily. She seemed tired but not exhausted, and she certainly didn't seem stressed out. Maybe it was easier for some women than others. Maybe women like his mother had just never wanted kids to begin with. Risa would never walk out on *her* child. He knew it in his soul.

Francie had awakened but seemed perfectly content to stare up at Simon as if she were learning everything about his features. He smiled at her and tickled her chin.

Just then, the door to the examining room area flew open and instead of a nurse, Simon saw a tall middle-aged man with graying hair and a wide smile. He nodded to Risa. "Come on in. Your husband can come back, too."

Instead of getting flustered, Risa stood and gathered Francie from Simon's arms. "He's not my husband. Simon is a friend."

The doctor's cheeks flushed. "Oh, I'm sorry."

Simon cleared his throat. "No problem. I helped deliver her." He felt as if he had to show some claim, some reason for being here.

"I see," Dr. Winslow said, but with a vacant expression that said he didn't see at all.

With Francie on her shoulder now, Risa captured the diaper bag, too, and went with the doctor down the hall.

When the door shut, Simon felt a bit shell-shocked. He'd told Risa he'd take this one step at a time. The first step suddenly seemed like a monumental one. He'd never thought of himself in the father role, never expected to even consider having kids. Just the responsibilities laid on a parent these days should make him head in the other direction. Again he thought about Francie's bright eyes on his face, her warm little body in her terry playsuit. He thought about the kisses he'd shared with Risa and how just remembering them aroused him.

He didn't know what the hell he was getting himself into, but he knew he was in it—and he wasn't backing out now.

As Risa nursed Francie that evening, she thought about how tenderly Simon had held her baby, how he'd proudly stated how he'd helped deliver her daughter, how he'd seen them both to the door and then invited Risa to go to the lake with him on Sunday. Cedar County Lake was a recreational area about a mile out of town where residents from the surrounding area could enjoy picnicking, boating, fishing and swimming. She couldn't believe how much she was looking forward to the day and to spending time with Simon again.

When the phone rang, she picked it up thinking it was probably Janetta checking in. It wasn't. It was her mother.

"Hi, honey. How'd the doctor's appointment go with Francie?"

"It went just fine. She's thriving—she's gained four ounces."

"Good for her. You never know about breast-feeding, whether they're getting enough or not."

"I'm giving her a supplemental bottle now and then, so she'll get used to it. I don't want you to have trouble feeding her when I go back to school in October."

"We won't have any trouble. She and I will get along fine. That reminds me. Lucy told me you have some books that Mary Lou would like. Can you bring them along on Sunday?"

Uh-oh. Land mine ahead. "About Sunday, Mama...I have other plans."

"What other plans? You know we always have dinner together on Sunday. It's a family thing."

"Yes, I know. But once in a while it's nice to break routine."

Her mother was silent for a few long moments, then she asked suspiciously, "Just *who* do you have plans with?"

Eluding her mother had never been easy and Risa didn't want to play games with her now. "Simon has asked me to go to the lake."

"Francie, too?"

"Yes, Francie, too."

Again there was a pause. "You know, if you're going to get involved with someone again, it shouldn't be a lawman."

"Would you approve of Simon if he had a trust fund?" Risa asked.

"Don't get smart with me, Risa."

"I'm not. But isn't that what you're looking at— Simon's salary?"

"That's one part of it. But just look at what he had to do. He rounded up those bank robbers. That's dangerous business. Do you want to be dating a man who could get killed?"

"I was married to a man who got killed."

There was a shocked silence. Finally Carmen responded, "I don't know what's gotten into you lately, Risa. You're not the same as you used to be."

"I'm trying to stand on my own two feet. That's important to me now."

"That's why you need to find someone like Todd who can give you security. Then you wouldn't have to worry about being so independent."

Risa had tried to break the bubble her mother had built around Todd before, but it had never worked. Now she simply said, "Todd gave me security, Mama, but he tried to control me. He didn't love me the way a husband should love a wife."

"You're exaggerating. You've *always* been too sensitive. You don't know how lucky you were to have Todd."

Somehow, Risa knew she could never have this conversation with her mother in person. It seemed easier over the phone, maybe because she had her full attention.

Instead of arguing, Risa asked, "Were you happy in your marriage?"

Time clicked along silently until her mother answered, "Your dad provided for me and all of you. That's what a husband should do."

"I want a lot more than that from a husband. I want tenderness and compassion and understanding."

"Your problem is that you're a romantic. I think you've read too many of those romance novels. Raising children is more expensive than it's ever been, and if you think you can do it on your own on a teacher's salary, you're sadly mistaken. Besides, if you were married to a man with enough money, you could stay home with Francie."

"We're never going to agree on this Mama. I wasn't happy with Todd. If I even consider getting married again, I'll have to be sure it's with the right man."

"You think Simon Blackstone is the right man?"

"I don't know. I don't know if I know him yet, but he seems honest and sincere."

"He has a reputation. He sees a lot of women."

"He's explained his reasons for that." She wasn't going to go into them with her mother. "He's not dating anyone else now."

She thought she heard her mother harumph. Finally Carmen let out a sigh. "Invite him along again on Sunday. Come and have dinner with us. You can go to the lake some other time."

"Mama…"

"It's important, Risa. Dom and Lucy are celebrating their anniversary next week and I'm going to have a cake for them. You shouldn't miss that."

She'd forgotten about Dom and Lucy's anniversary, but she didn't know what Simon would think about going along. "I accepted Simon's invitation, and I don't want to cancel on him. But I'll ask him if he'd like to come to dinner. If he says yes, I'll call you."

"And if you don't call, I'm just supposed to accept

that my youngest daughter doesn't want to be part of this family anymore?"

"I'll call you either way. No matter what I decide or what Simon decides, I'll always be part of the Lombardi family. I love you, Mama, but I'm not as attached to tradition as you are."

There was a very long silence. "If you don't come to dinner Sunday, it will be just the beginning. After a while you'll stop coming at all."

So *that* was her mother's fear. "That's not true. I'll never be too busy to spend time with you and Lucy and Dom and Janetta."

"Even if you start seeing that…sheriff?"

"Even if I start seeing Simon, there will be plenty of room in my life for everyone."

"We'll see," Carmen replied as if the wisdom of the ages made her all-knowing.

Risa had to smile. Her mother would never change. Maybe that wasn't a bad thing because her family was definitely the one constant in her life.

Simon agreed to go along with Risa to her family's for dinner on Sunday because…

He wasn't exactly sure why. He wanted to be alone with Risa yet when he was, his self-control was at a premium. He wasn't sure she was ready for more than a few kisses. He wasn't sure *he* was ready for more, either…and for everything it would mean to his life.

When they arrived at the Lombardi house, Carmen again gave him the once-over. She was obviously resigned to his presence and asked if he wanted something to drink before dinner. Before he could reply, his cell phone rang. When he checked the caller ID, he saw it was one of his deputies.

Excusing himself, he took the call in the kitchen. "What's up, Anson?"

"Vandals again. They spray-painted the water tower. I thought you'd want to know."

He *did* want to know. He just wished the call hadn't come at this moment. "I'll meet you at the water tower in five minutes."

"Trouble?" Carmen asked as she and Risa came into the kitchen.

"Afraid so. I'm going to have to check it out."

"Will you be back for dinner?" Risa's tone said she'd be disappointed if he wasn't.

"I don't know how long this will take, probably about an hour. I don't want to hold up the meal. You go ahead and eat. I'll stop back here after I check out what's going on."

Carmen glanced at Risa then looked over at Simon. "I'll keep something warm for you. You make sure you stop back here so you get something good to eat."

"I'll make sure I do that." He wanted to give Risa a good-bye kiss, but with her mother watching, the seeds of acceptance growing, he didn't want to upset her. So instead, he took Risa's hand, gave it a slight squeeze, and then went to his truck.

It was an hour and a half later when he returned, and the Lombardi family was having dessert. There was an empty chair across from Risa and next to David.

When Lucy motioned to it, she said, "Mama kept a little bit of everything warm."

Risa was already pulling a platter from the oven. When she set the plate in front of him, she smiled. "Braciola and scalloped potatoes." The braciola was rolled meat stuffed with cheese, and it looked delicious.

After he took a bite, he felt Carmen watching him. "It's great. It must have taken a lot of time to prepare."

"I got up early this morning," she admitted. "I love to cook. It gives me something to do." She added with a smile, "Until I have Francie to take care of."

"You're going back to school when it starts August 16?" he asked Risa. That was a little over a week away.

"I'm taking time off and going back in October. I have to," she said simply, and he was sorry he'd brought it up.

Especially when Carmen asked, "What do you mean, you *have* to? Todd had no other relatives. Everything went to you."

"Todd left me bills, Mama. That's why I moved in with Janetta. I need to go back to teaching to keep up with paying them."

Her mother looked stunned, and Simon didn't know if he'd opened a can of worms or done some good. Maybe it was time Carmen realized the realities of Risa's life. He still wanted to know about Risa's marriage, but she'd have to trust him to tell him about that and he wasn't sure she did yet.

Cutting through the tension, Risa pointed to the gift bag sitting on the counter. "Didn't you say you bought Francie a present?"

"I almost forgot," Carmen said, managing a smile, looking as if she were still trying to absorb what Risa had told her. Holding Francie in the crook of one arm, Carmen picked up the bag and set it in front of her youngest daughter.

"She'll grow into it," she said with a wink.

Suddenly David pushed his chair back from the table. "I'm going outside."

"Honey, it's hot out there. Don't you want to wait and see what Risa's opening?" Carmen asked.

He swiped his hand at the package. "Nah, it's baby stuff. I don't care. I'm going to practice pitching against the garage."

David had been silent ever since Simon had sat beside him. When he put his hands on the table to push his chair back, Simon noticed something...something that bothered him.

While Risa was opening the bag with the tissue paper and everyone's eyes were on her, he said to David, "It looks as if you've been painting." There were telltale signs of red paint under his fingernails.

Looking flustered for a moment, the boy quickly recovered. "I paint airplane models. I spilled a bottle of paint. When I cleaned it up, I got it all over me."

That explanation was plausible, Simon knew, but he also knew there could be another explanation. Whoever had sprayed the water tower had done it with red paint. There were no witnesses, nothing left behind, no clues. Whoever these kids were, they were good. Maybe later he could ask Lucy if David had been home last night. If he'd spent the night with a friend...

Risa pushed back the pastel pink tissue and reached inside the bag. She drew out a dress, pink, too, with more ruffles than he could count.

"She'll look so pretty in it," Carmen decided proudly. "They had some little patent leather shoes, but I didn't think she'd keep them on. See the hair band?"

A baby hair band with pink ruffles and a bow attached on the side accompanied the dress.

"It's adorable, Mama. Thank you." Then Risa hugged and kissed her mother. Simon could see there wasn't the enthusiasm in Risa's eyes that had been in Carmen's. Something about that dress bothered her and he wondered why.

Fifteen minutes later everyone was in the yard except for Risa, who was nursing Francie inside before she laid her in the small portable crib Carmen had set up to let her take a nap. Simon missed Risa's presence when she wasn't by his side. He couldn't remember ever missing a woman like that before.

To distract himself from disturbing thoughts he still wasn't comfortable with, he ambled over to Lucy who was tossing a large vinyl ball to Mary Lou under the shade of the elm. "Need a third?" he asked.

Mary Lou, who had the ball just then, rolled it to him, making the decision for all of them.

Lucy laughed. "She loves to play with somebody besides me. I always do the same old, same old."

"I imagine it's hard to keep kids occupied. When Risa and I were planning our public safety campaign, she told me their attention span is about fifteen minutes on a good day."

"That's true for the younger ones. David stays with one activity a lot longer now."

Lucy always liked to talk about her kids, so getting her to chat about David didn't seem to be a problem or raise any suspicions. "David told me he likes to paint model airplanes."

"And cars and boats. What a mess."

"Is he into computers yet?"

"Oh, yeah. He was in his room all evening last night playing those games. He says he has friends he meets online."

Apparently David was home last night, but just to make sure, Simon asked, "Does he sleep over at friends' houses much? I hear kids like to do that."

"Now and then. A couple of weeks ago he spent the weekend with a friend."

"I guess he has a gang he runs around with."

"His teacher tells me he likes to hang out with some older boys. I don't know if that's good or bad."

Simon didn't know, either, and it depended on whether the older boys were a positive influence or a negative influence.

When Simon rolled Mary Lou the ball, it went past her and she scurried after it.

Wiping her brow, Lucy straightened. "Whew, it's hot out here. I think I'll get something to drink. Want some iced tea?"

"Sounds good."

It was close to dusk when Simon helped Risa take Francie and her paraphernalia back home. All evening

Risa was quieter than usual. Did Sunday dinners with her family do that? Or was something else bothering her?

Francie had had a fussy spell at the Lombardi's but now was sleeping peacefully again. Simon carried her car seat with her in it into the living room.

Once he'd placed it on the sofa, Risa unfastened her daughter, scooped her up and laid her in the bassinet. Then she bent and gave her a kiss on the forehead. "Sometimes I still can't believe she's mine."

"Your mom sure dotes on her. She can't wait to baby-sit when you go back to teaching."

"I know," Risa said with a troubled look.

"What's wrong?"

Straightening a ruffle on the bassinet's cover, Risa answered, "It's Mama's attitude towards women and men and little girls and little boys. She puts them into compartments and heaven forbid they should try to stretch out of them. I'm worried about Francie growing up with that."

She'd set the gift bag her mother had given her on the sofa. Lifting it, she took out the small frilly dress. "This is adorable and I can't wait until Francie grows into it."

"But?"

"But Mama is going to want her to wear patent leather shoes and frilly outfits all the time. She'll want her to take ballet lessons, too."

Simon couldn't help but smile. "Is there anything wrong with that?"

"That depends. If Francie has a talent for dancing

and she wants to be a ballerina, if she loves frilly dresses, there's no problem. But if she's a tomboy, loves jeans, wants to go out for Little League or be a fighter pilot, I want her to have the opportunity for that, too. I want her to know she can do anything and doesn't have to be restricted by what other people think are men's and women's roles."

Only the table lamp dimly lit the living room. There was an intimacy about it as shadows wrapped around them, and they stood looking down at Risa's daughter. Simon thought he'd kept an admirable distance from Risa the whole day when all he'd wanted to do was tug her into his arms, taste her sweetness all over again and get lost in thoughts of what they could do together.

Now he moved closer to her and nudged her around to face him. "*You* are her mother, Risa. *You're* going to be her main influence and her main teacher. If she learns from you that she can be whatever she wants to be, you don't have to worry about your mother's influence, or your sister's influence, or *anybody's* influence."

"But if she's with Mama all day everyday until she goes to school…"

"She'll be with you every evening and every night, on weekends and days off and all through the summer. And if she's as smart as I think she'll be, she'll soon realize your mother's world is very narrow, but the one you want to show her is very wide. I think you're worrying too much."

A shadow crossed Risa's face that he didn't understand. "My worries are legitimate," she protested with a cautious expression now.

"Yes, they are. But I think maybe you're focusing on them because you don't want to focus on the chemistry between us."

The defensiveness left her face then and her voice was almost a whisper. "Sometimes I think you see too much. That scares me, Simon...along with the chemistry."

He could see she was struggling to understand the bond growing between them, to understand the fire that licked at them both whenever they touched or kissed. With sudden insight, he knew if he didn't back off, she'd run.

He should forget about this woman who had a child...who needed more than scorching desire from a man who wasn't sure he wanted to be a husband or a dad.

Difficult as it was, he didn't take her into his arms. He didn't kiss her. He stepped away. "Thanks for inviting me along today."

"You enjoyed yourself?"

"I did. You've got to understand something, Risa. Your family has its quirks, but you have a family who cares about each other. You're fortunate in that."

Her cheeks reddened slightly. "Yes, I guess I am."

"I'll let you get settled for the night. I can see myself out."

When she nodded, he wondered if she was relieved he didn't suggest another date.

He wasn't relieved, he was just unnerved by Risa and Francie and how they tilted his life.

When he left her house, he realized he needed some

space, too—a whole heck of a lot of it. If he truly got involved with Risa Lombardi Parker, nothing would ever be the same.

Chapter Seven

It was a hot night. Thunder rumbled in the distance and heat lightning flashed in the sky. At 2 a.m., Simon was more restless than he'd ever been and staying cooped up in an air-conditioned house after being in an air-conditioned office all day made him feel like the proverbial caged lion.

So he sat on his patio, chair tipped back, his legs crossed on another chair not three feet away as he waited for the first fat raindrops to fall. They could use more rain but that didn't mean they'd get it. That rumbling could be a false alarm. The heat lightning would eventually fade into the first rays of dawn, a lot of commotion without a satisfying conclusion.

Were the rumblings in his libido, the flash of heat whenever he was around Risa, preparatory phenomena, too? For the past week and a half he'd stayed away from her, hoping, wondering, believing if he did, images of her would fade from his life and his dreams. He'd been dead wrong.

Considering everything that had happened the past few weeks, he'd decided she wasn't ready for an affair *or* an involvement if she couldn't even tell him about her marriage. At first, he hadn't thought he was interested in anything past a tumble in the dark. Yet when he thought of Risa, he thought of Francie. He imagined the pride he'd feel watching Francie grow. In the swirl of all of it, he remembered how his mother had loved his father, how she'd pined for him when he was in prison, how she'd grieved in despair after he'd died. All these years Simon had told himself if that's what love did to a person, he wanted no part of it. All these years, he'd believed his road would be a hell of a lot easier with no strings. Strings got all knotted up, tangled and tore.

The scent of the damp, pre-rain night, the cloudy gray sky, the swish of amur maple leaves overhead filled his senses until suddenly he went on alert. The light came on in Risa's kitchen, the back door opened, and he heard Francie crying.

He should stay put and mind his own business. He should forget he was her neighbor, forget he was the first person ever to hold Francie, forget Risa aroused him more than any woman he'd ever met.

Fat chance.

Francie was crying in earnest now, and Risa was murmuring to her. Every sound carried in the void of night and when he heard a jangle of keys, heard the sound of metal on pavement, he untilted his chair, walked to the edge of the hedge and crossed into Risa's yard.

"What are you doing?" he asked as he saw her set Francie's car seat on the walk where she crouched down.

Her gasp of surprise made him swear.

Then he said, "I didn't mean to scare you. I was sitting on my patio and heard you...heard *her.*"

As Francie's cries rent the air, Risa scooped up her keys from the concrete path then lifted the car seat once more. "I have to go to the discount store. It's open all night. I ran out of diapers. She's been really fussy the past couple of days and I lost track."

Under the glow of the back porch light, he could see Risa looked harried. She'd tied her hair back in a ponytail and loose strands wisped around her face. Under the harsh light, he could see shadows under her eyes and she looked thinner, maybe too thin.

"What's going on, Risa? You look as if you haven't slept in a week."

As Francie's crying seemed to fill the backyard, Risa took the pacifier from the car seat and wiggled it into Francie's mouth. The baby sucked on it.

"I haven't slept much. Janetta was supposed to be home but something happened to the computer network and she had to stay. Francie's had colic for the past day and a half. I really don't have time to talk, Simon. I not only need diapers but drops the doctor said might help the colic."

Without hesitation, he took Francie's car seat from her.

"What are you doing?"

"I'm going to drive you."

She tugged the car seat back into her arms. "Don't start, Simon. You've come to my rescue one too many times already. I don't know why you think you have to rush over here and take over…" Her voice trembled, and she bit her lower lip.

Even with the scare Risa had had with false labor, the intensity of her contractions when they'd finally come, the pain of the real labor and delivery, he'd never seen her this close to tears. He'd heard women's hormones didn't settle down right away after the birth of a baby and postpartum depression affected more women than anyone imagined. Heck, sleep deprivation alone was bad enough. Add hormonal shifts to it—

Something told him Risa didn't want to be consoled or coddled. In fact either would only make matters worse.

"If you don't let me drive you, I might have to arrest you."

"What?"

"You're under the influence, Risa."

"I haven't had—"

"No, you haven't had anything to drink. You're under the influence of a baby. She's needed you twenty-four hours a day since she's been born. You've taken care of her alone and done a damn good job of it. But you're in no condition to drive to a store in the middle of the night. I really wouldn't want to be called to a fender-bender or something worse because you didn't have the good sense to let me drive."

"You wouldn't be called to anything. You're not on duty."

"I'm *always* on duty. I'm on call twenty-four hours a day and because of the well-oiled gossip highway in Cedar Corners, you can bet I'd get a call if anything happened concerning you."

They were both remembering her visit to his office and the comments made then.

"I'm tired of feeling indebted to you, Simon," she said wearily.

He could see that really troubled her. "You're not indebted to me for anything."

As she started to protest, he asked, "If I needed a ride to the store in the middle of the night, would you take me?"

"You know I would."

"All right then. Be practical about this. We're both awake. If you drive yourself, I'll sit over there on that patio and worry until you get back."

"You'll worry?" She seemed genuinely surprised by that, and he wanted to haul her into his arms and kiss her senseless.

Instead, he just answered succinctly, "Yes," and kept his hands to himself.

She seemed to be wavering, and he took advantage of her indecision and held his hand out for her keys. "We can take your car so you don't feel indebted for gas, too."

At that, she almost smiled, then dropped the keys into his hand.

Forty-five minutes later, Risa had given Francie some of the drops and she'd seemed more comfortable on the ride home. As she opened the back door to let Simon bring Francie inside, she didn't think she'd ever been so tired in her life. She couldn't remember when she'd last had more than two and a half hours of uninterrupted sleep. When she'd first brought Francie home, she'd been handling it just fine. Now the buildup was wearing her down.

"I need to change her, and she'll probably be ready to nurse soon."

Simon set Francie's car seat on the kitchen table. "Her eyes are open. She looks as if she's ready to have a good time if the colic doesn't act up again."

"I'm hoping she soon starts sleeping through one of the night feedings. You were right about me being too tired to drive tonight. I was counting on Janetta being home by now."

"Maybe your mother could come over and stay a few nights and give you a break."

"I don't want to ask her, but I might have to. I did say I wanted to handle my life on my own, didn't I?"

"You *are* handling your life on your own. Needing a bit of assistance doesn't make you a bad mother. It's abdicating all responsibility that does that."

As she set the drops the doctor had suggested on the counter, she thought about Simon's childhood. "How old were you when you went to live with your aunt?"

"I was nine. Like any kid, I could never really understand why my mother left. But seeing you taking care of Francie alone, it hits the ball home. It's damn difficult."

Risa could see that this was something that had torn

Simon up, that had colored his childhood and made its mark on his adulthood. Gently now, she offered, "Just because your mother gave you to your aunt to raise, doesn't mean she didn't love you. In fact, it was probably the hardest decision she ever had to make. She might have done it because she loved you a lot. Sometimes love means letting go as well as holding on."

The nerve in Simon's jaw worked. Finally, he reached out, clasped Risa's shoulder, and brought her closer.

After the day she and Simon had spent at her mother's, Risa had expectantly waited for him to call or visit. When he hadn't, she'd decided he'd lost interest. If he was that kind of man, it was best if she didn't see him again. Yet she'd missed him...more than she ever thought she would. She found herself peering out the side window to catch a glimpse of him as he strode up his back walk. She'd watched for his lights to go on and his lights to go out, imagining him dating women who were more beautiful than she was, who could trust him because he was easy to trust, who could go to bed with him because they simply wanted to have fun.

He didn't seem to bring anyone home. That didn't mean he hadn't gotten involved. That didn't mean—

"What's going on in that head of yours?" he asked huskily.

"I wondered if in the last week or so, you might have found someone to date."

His large hand cupped her cheek as the scent of man and soap surrounded her. "For some insane reason, I can't seem to concentrate on other women. You've gotten under my skin, Risa. Have I gotten under yours?"

It would be silly to say no, to push him away, to go about her life without him. She felt connected to Simon in a way she'd never felt connected to another man. It terrified her sometimes. She didn't want the connection, yet something about it felt inexorably right, too.

"Yes, you have."

He looked pleased and then worried as his thumb gently traced the skin under her eyes. "You're exhausted, aren't you?"

"I just need a couple hours of sleep. After I feed her, hopefully I'll get them."

"How about if you get more than a couple of hours?"

"I don't think that's going to happen until she's older." She managed a smile.

Nodding to the clean bottles in the sink drainer, he asked, "She takes a bottle?"

"Yes."

"Good. Then you go to bed. I'll keep her company and feed her."

"You have to go to work tomorrow."

"I can take the morning off. I'm the sheriff, remember?"

"You've done enough, Simon."

He brought his face very close to hers until his lips were almost brushing hers. "Not nearly enough," he murmured as he gently kissed her. It wasn't hot or hard, but it was breathtakingly sensual.

When he broke it off, he suggested, "Go to bed. I'll bunk on the couch. If Francie doesn't like me taking care of her, I'll let you know...or *she* will."

Having Simon there in the house in the middle of the

night with her gave Risa a sense of safety she'd never had before. The thought of getting more than a couple of hours of sleep was a gift she couldn't turn down.

"You know the payback on this should be at least a week of home-cooked meals," she offered lightly.

"Maybe I'd rather have something else for payback," he said in that deep dark voice that gave her shivers. This time she didn't want to run from the sensuality in it. This time she thought about welcoming Simon and everything he wanted to give her.

Yet she couldn't even think about that for another few weeks, and he knew that.

Before she could make too much of his remark, she said, "I have spare milk in a jar in the refrigerator. Just set the bottle in hot water to warm it..."

He turned her around and gave her a little push toward the stairs. "I've seen you do it. The clock's ticking. Go get some sleep while you can."

As Risa mounted the stairs, she took a last glimpse back into the kitchen. She knew even if she slept, her dreams would be filled with Simon.

When Risa awakened, the sun was bright, falling through her bedroom window. Sitting up, she smelled coffee and something even better though she wasn't sure what it was. Glancing at the clock on her nightstand, she saw that it was 10 a.m. She hadn't slept that well since long before Francie was born.

The clatter of dishes in the kitchen urged her to hurry. She took a quick shower, towel-dried her hair, and dressed in a purple-and-pink-flowered shorts and top set. With her feet still bare, she hurried down the stairs to say good morning to her daughter and to Simon.

When she entered the kitchen, Simon was flipping pancakes off the griddle onto a platter, singing some sort of lullaby to her daughter—an easy tune about hummingbirds and raindrops. Francie was half dozing, half awake, sitting in her car seat on the table, facing Simon.

He was dressed in his uniform looking as handsome and sexy as ever. How had he accomplished that? Had he left Francie alone downstairs…

The last pancake stacked on the platter, Simon turned toward her. "I took Francie along next door to get my pancake mix and the uniform. I didn't leave her alone, if that's what you're thinking."

She felt a blush steal over her cheeks. How did the man know her so well?

Going over to Francie, she picked her up and saw she had a fresh change of clothes. "I guess you changed her, too?"

"I figured if I needed a change, she would." His grin was as sardonic as his tone.

"I didn't think you'd attempt it since you haven't been around babies much."

"It's not as hard as I thought it might be. I guess she likes me."

Settling her baby back into the carrier, Risa decided that that wasn't only true of her daughter. "You shouldn't have let me sleep so late."

"I was going to call you. Come on and eat before these get cold. I have to leave in about ten minutes."

"I thought you were taking off this morning."

"So did I, but I got a call about an hour ago. Some vandals have been defacing property. They struck again, this time painting a few road signs. But we've got an eyewitness now. Anson already took preliminary notes. I'm going to follow up."

She found herself feeling sorry that he would be leaving. It was an odd feeling. She'd never missed Todd when he'd left. It had almost been a relief. But she liked having Simon around.

The idea of caring deeply for him terrified her. What if she was wrong again? What if his kindness and caring and gentleness weren't really a part of him? What if his take-charge attitude was his dominant characteristic? What if the rest was just a cover to get her to like him, to get her into bed with him?

"Risa?"

She realized she was still standing there, and the pancakes were cooling on the table. Pulling out a chair, she settled herself in it.

He took a seat next to her as she turned Francie's carrier to face her.

Seconds later, Simon clasped her arm, and she found herself staring into his blue eyes.

"I have about five minutes to chow down. But before I do, I want to ask you something."

His calloused fingers were hot on her arm. Her insides trembled from anticipation, being close to him, from wanting to be even closer.

"Do you think Lucy would watch Francie tomorrow evening for a few hours? Or maybe your mother?"

"Why?"

"Because I'd like to take you to the lake. Just the two of us. Not that I don't love Francie's company..." He glanced at the baby and grinned, then his expression became serious once more. "But I think you could use a break and I'd like the time alone with you. We could take a picnic for a late supper and swim."

His eyes told her that he might have something more in mind than swimming. Did *she?*

A vision popped into her head of her feeding Simon a luxuriant strawberry. She felt herself grow hot, and she took a deep breath. She wasn't going to be a coward. Life was about grabbing each moment and enjoying it to the fullest. She wanted so badly to teach her daughter to do that, too, so she'd better practice herself.

"I'd like to go to the lake with you. I'll call Lucy and see if she's free."

Simon leaned back then and she was almost disappointed. But the flare of desire in his eyes told her she wouldn't be disappointed tomorrow, not if she had the courage to embrace whatever was growing between them.

When Simon looked over Anson's notes, his gut told him what he was going to find when he'd finished this investigation. And he had to decide how he was going to deal with it. But he wanted to interview the witness himself and make sure of the facts before he took the next step. Mr. Truhenny lived in the brick two-story on the corner where the road sign had been painted.

The older man had welcomed Simon with an offer of coffee even though the temperature was already in the mid-nineties. Simon had declined and now stood looking out the man's picture window in his living room. There was an unobstructed view of the stop sign, and the street light was positioned directly above it.

"You say it was around midnight when you saw the boys at the stop sign?" He turned back to look at Mr. Truhenny who'd settled himself in his easy chair. Simon guessed he was around seventy-five.

"I'd just come down for a bowl of cereal. Couldn't sleep. That's usual these days. I heard kids laughing. That's what brought me out here to the living room."

Mr. Truhenny was elderly and his eyesight could be failing. Simon had to tactfully cover that base, too. "You told my deputy you could see the boys clearly."

"Sure could. I had cataract surgery five years ago, both eyes. Since then, I got twenty-twenty vision. So I didn't mistake what I saw."

"Would you mind telling me what you saw?"

"Checking your deputy's notes, are you? I don't mind. It's nice to have some company for a change."

Simon realized that, as with a lot of retired folk, Mr. Truhenny was lonely. He waited for the man's story.

"I saw four boys," the older man explained. "They all had bicycles. The tallest one was Joey Martin. I recognized him right away. That blond hair of his, spiked up like it got no place to go. He caused some trouble in my backyard last summer. Used my fence as a hurdle, just for the fun of it. Jumping back and forth to see if he could. I would have liked to slap a paintbrush in his hand instead. He could have gotten hurt on those pickets! Anyway, he was one of them."

Okay, Simon thought, *the first identification is certain.*

"The second boy was Cap Grayson's grandson," Mr. Truhenny continued. "He's a redhead and usually runs around with Joey. The other two I didn't know, but I got a good look at their bikes. One of them had a license plate with 'Mike' spelled out on it. The other fella had dark brown hair, cut real short on the sides, long on the top."

At that description, Simon's stomach sank. David Lombardi's hair was cut in that style.

"Anything else about him you noticed?"

"Yeah, he had a green bike, one of those expensive racing numbers. There was one of those bandanna things tied to the handlebars. Don't know what that means, but I'm sure it's something."

Simon closed his notebook on both his scratchings and Anson's descriptions. "Thank you for all your help, Mr. Truhenny. If these are the kids we're after, I'll see what I can do about teaching them vandalism isn't the road to good citizenship."

Although Simon would have preferred to leave right away, again the older man offered him something to drink. This time Simon accepted the coffee and listened to Mr. Truhenny's observations about the neighborhood.

As Simon drove to the middle school a half hour later—school had been in session less than a week—he turned the situation over in his head, deciding to find out what the boys' motivation was before he doled out punishment. Simon wanted to teach them all a lesson, but he wasn't going to make a mountain out of a mole-hill, either.

Fifteen minutes later, he stood in the principal's of-fice with the four boys. Not only did Truhenny's ob-servations match David Lombardi's description, but Simon remembered seeing the boy's bike parked at his grandmother's house. It was green with a bandanna tied on the handlebars. After asking a few questions, there wasn't a doubt that these four ran together. And when Simon told them he had an eyewitness, they caved. David wouldn't look him in the eye.

He could see at once that Joey Martin was the risk-taker and the leader. The other three were followers.

"What were you trying to accomplish?" he asked Joey now.

The boy gave one of those teenage almost-shrugs that frustrated adults so. "I dunno. Just needed some-thing to do. There's no place to have fun in this town."

Unfortunately, that was true. There was a playground with swings and a sandbox for little kids, but nothing for this intermediate age.

"Even if there was a place you kids could go to shoot hoops or play foozball or whatever, it wouldn't be open after midnight."

The redhead mumbled, "Maybe if we had some-thing to do in the summer and after school, we wouldn't need to do something at midnight."

"What do you think would have happened if your parents found out you were gone at midnight?"

All four boys looked down at the floor.

Now David's gaze did meet Simon's. "Please don't

tell my parents, Sheriff Blackstone. They'll tell my grandmother. She'll have a heart attack!"

David might have been dramatizing, but not by too much. "Why don't you want me to tell your parents, David? Because they'll punish you?"

"I don't know if they will or not," he said honestly. "I don't want them to…I don't want them to be disappointed in me."

"Are you afraid they won't trust you again?"

Looking thoroughly upset by the idea, David nodded.

Simon knew he could play this two different ways. He could haul them all down to the station, call in their parents, make a big deal of everything that had happened. Years ago that kind of scene might have worked. The boys would have been embarrassed, straightened up, and that would have been the end of it. But now, he didn't know if the parents would mete out punishment. These boys could turn defiant and cause even more trouble. Maybe it would be better to get them on his side to try to work with him rather than against him.

"I could put all four of you in jail for defacing public property."

The boys' eyes grew wide.

"But I can't see a lot of purpose in that. So here's the deal. I won't put you in jail, and I won't call your parents. In return, the four of you have to meet me at Mr. Truhenny's house early on Saturday. You're going to paint his fence. If you do a good job, I'll consider your debt to the community paid."

He saw relief changing their morose expressions. Attempting to win them over further, he went on, "Along with that, you have to agree to stay out of trouble and not sneak out at night. In the meantime, I'll try to rally support for a youth center. Maybe we could get it going at the middle school or the high school. It would give you someplace to go and something to do."

David smiled at Simon for the first time since he'd known him. "That sounds great. Maybe Mr. Robson, the science teacher, could plan some science projects. I heard he does neat stuff with the high school kids."

David had just confirmed what Simon had guessed. He was a smart kid with too much time on his hands and needed direction and supervised activity.

"I'll talk to the principal about it and the school board members. Maybe we can get a program worked up soon...and maybe even a year-round community center."

He eyed each boy one at a time. "Let's make something clear. If you're not at Mr. Truhenny's at seven-thirty on Saturday morning, I will come looking for you in the sheriff's car. Got it?"

All four boys solemnly nodded.

Chapter Eight

Carrying the insulated rectangular cooler that held their picnic, Simon glanced at Risa. She was dressed in pink and white tonight. Her blouse was striped, buttoned down the front and tied at her midriff. It met the band of her pink shorts that stopped mid-thigh. He could see the shadow of her bathing suit underneath the cotton, and his pulse raced faster every time he thought about seeing her in it. Not even the phone call he'd received last night about an unexpected job offer could swerve his focus from her.

The sky was as blue as cornflowers and a few puffy white clouds floated over the late-day sun. Risa toted a small duffel bag with her towels and other paraphernalia. Her hair swung along her cheek as they walked, and he longed to brush it back. He longed to make this evening more than a simple date. He'd never thought beyond the evening with a woman before. That still unsettled him. But *not* seeing Risa again, going back to being simply neighbors, unsettled him even more.

As they walked through a field of long grass and wild flowers, Risa bent to pick small yellow ones. She didn't ask him to stop, just picked the flowers and hurried to keep in step again.

"It's only a little bit farther," he said.

"I don't think I've ever been on this side of the lake before."

Cedar County Lake was about a mile in width. On the east side, there was a more manicured beach, bathrooms, and changing stalls. But Simon was leading Risa to the west side. He wanted to be away from people tonight...alone with Risa. So he'd brought her to a spot where he often came for solitude.

The field gave way to a band of pines. Simon stepped ahead of Risa as they walked on layers of fragrant needles. The temperature was cooler under the trees, and the hush and whisper of branches blowing in the wind slowed Simon's pace as he checked over his shoulder to make sure Risa was following. She was, though she seemed to be taking it all in, too.

After a short while, they poked through the trees and grass that gently sloped down to the lake. There wasn't a person in sight.

Choosing a spot under a tall oak, he lowered the cooler to the ground and then spread the blanket that had been folded on top of it.

Risa watched him, and he got hot as he felt her gaze on him when he spread the blanket.

She unfolded one corner that didn't seem to want to

straighten. "What do you want to do first?" she asked with a look that told him she was unsure about being with him here tonight.

"Let's take a swim. Then if a thunderstorm comes up, we can always grab the food and eat in the car."

In August, afternoon and evening storms often developed. Besides, a swim might relax them both. He was wound as tight as Risa for a multitude of reasons—the mere fact of just being with her, the distraction of thinking about that job offer, the situation with David. He'd briefly considered telling her about the vandalism, but that would be going back on his word to the boy. He was hoping a good dose of hard work and the pact he'd made with the kids would curb their search for adventure in all the wrong places.

It was obvious Risa didn't want to strip off her clothes in front of him. She nodded to a clump of cedars. "I'll take off my clothes over there."

Modesty in this day and age surprised Simon, but he liked the idea of it and admired Risa even more.

He had no qualms about dropping his cutoffs to the blanket, revealing his black trunks. Then he removed his T-shirt. He'd worn moccasins, no socks, and now left the shoes at the edge of the blanket. Striding toward the lake, he decided to cool off while he waited for Risa.

The wait seemed like forever but then she was standing there in a hot pink suit looking as if she hadn't had a baby a month before.

Although the water was cool, she didn't hesitate to walk right in. Wading up to him, she smiled. "It feels wonderful."

The water where they were standing was about four and a half feet deep and skimmed the crest of her breasts. Simon felt himself grow hard in spite of the cool water. "You look wonderful."

Her cheeks grew rosy. "I started exercising again and I'm back to my pre-Francie weight. But I don't feel the same."

Although he wouldn't embarrass her by saying it, he knew what she meant. Her breasts were fuller, her hips just a bit curvier. "You went through a life-altering experience."

"I guess that's part of it. My body changed. My mindset changed."

"It was hard for you to leave Francie tonight, wasn't it?" He'd seen the look on her face when they'd left.

She was quick to assure him, "I wanted to come. But I felt as if I were leaving part of me behind."

"An invisible cord will always connect the two of you." He understood that even though he wasn't sure a man could really know exactly what it meant.

"I've been working on projects for when I go back to teaching in October. I think I might try to do tutoring until then."

"You don't want to go back, do you?"

"I love teaching. But I'd rather be with Francie more."

"Your mom will take good care of her."

"I know she will. She'll spoil her completely."

Last rays of sun caught the red highlights in Risa's hair. Her dark eyes sparkled with amusement, with her joy in her daughter and her pleasure in the evening. The sounds of faraway laughter rode on the wind, an outboard engine started up, birds chirped in the trees. All of it was a backdrop to his growing desire for her.

She was standing less than a foot from him and now he couldn't keep from reaching out toward her, from gently clasping her shoulders, from taking a few steps forward. "I can't believe we're finally alone."

"We've been alone before," she said softly.

"Not like this."

"Simon…"

It was a warning but one he wasn't going to heed, not tonight. "Don't be afraid," he murmured as he took her face between his hands.

As heat closed in an electric circle between them, neither of them could deny the chemistry that had tempted and taunted for the past six weeks. If there had been any hesitation in Risa, he would have backed off. He sensed there was fear. But it was a fear of the unknown…not a fear of him…not a fear of what they were going to do. Risa was as feminine as a woman could get and if she came alive for him sexually, he knew they'd both get burned. Yet right now it was a burning he craved.

His lips brushed hers as if he was just saying hello. He felt her tremble and he tried it again. When he nibbled on her upper lip, she moaned softly. His hands left her face and he encircled her, bringing her close. Bathing suits weren't much of a barrier as he opened his mouth over hers, brought her into him and let her feel how much he wanted her.

A small gasp escaped from her.

He broke the kiss to murmur in her ear, "I know it's too soon. That's okay."

His hands went up her back and he was so tempted to slide the straps of her bathing suit down over her shoulders. Yet he knew Risa, knew she wouldn't be pushed or coerced or led. He wanted her to need the physical contact as much as he did.

With the last swirl of his tongue around her mouth, he broke away, managed to smile, and said, "We'd better cool off."

She looked a bit dazed, and that was okay. If she wanted more, he'd give it to her next time. Stroking one hand down her hair, he grinned, ducked under the surface and swam into deeper water.

When Simon swam away, Risa stood there feeling disappointed, aroused...empty. It was so odd. She'd expected never to need a man in her life again, never to want a man in her life. But Simon...whenever he wasn't around, she missed him. Whenever he kissed her, she wanted more. Maybe he hadn't been around babies much, but he'd learned fast and he was so good with Francie.

However, there were questions in her heart. If they became seriously involved, would he change? Would his take-charge attitude become an issue of control? Would he try to convince her to do what *he* wanted, never mind what *she* wanted?

She told herself for tonight she was going to forget about all of it and simply have fun. It had been a long time since she'd done that and she suddenly knew that with Simon, she could.

Diving into the deeper water, she swam toward him,

choosing to live in the moment for maybe the first time in her life.

Most of the time, Risa had trouble taking her eyes off of Simon. His shoulders were broad enough to block out the descending sun, and his wet hair over his dark brows intrigued her. His chest hair caught water droplets and glistened, emphasizing the flat tautness of his stomach and his black bathing trunks. Whenever she looked at him, her imagination went wild. The intensity in his blue eyes and the silver sparks told her he was having some of the same thoughts she was.

They played like two kids, racing, trying to dunk each other, floating on their backs.

Suddenly, an insistent beeping rode on the breeze.

Simon swore. "I'd better get that."

He held out his hand to her as his feet touched the bottom of the lake. "Come on. We should eat supper anyway."

"You might have to go into the office."

"Not if I can help it," he muttered.

Risa followed him to the shore and toweled off while he took the call.

Stepping a few feet away from the blanket, he listened intently. She heard him say, "No, that doesn't make my decision easier. A bonus isn't necessarily what I'm after. You told me you'd give me two weeks to consider it. I'll get back to you when I've made a decision or by the deadline." Then he ended the call and dropped the phone onto the blanket, looking troubled.

Risa finished toweling off and sat on the blanket near the cooler. "Was that your office?"

Silent for a few moments, he grabbed a towel,

quickly used it and came over to sit beside her. "No," he finally answered. "That was a man who owns a structural engineering firm in Tulsa. He first called me last night."

Her heart started beating faster, not only from Simon's proximity this time. "What did he want?"

"He offered me a job as head of security for his company. They have a research and development plant as well as inspectors that do home inspections."

"Research and development?"

"They're experimenting with new materials to build with—types of homes from solar to those using bales of straw for the walls. He explained some of it—also mentioned there were patents pending. That's why he needs security. He saw the clip on the news of the press conference."

"And his firm is in Tulsa?"

"Yep. He wants me to go out there and tour it."

"I couldn't help but hear something about a bonus?"

"The salary is a figure I never thought I'd see. He just added something to sweeten the deal."

Had she just found Simon only to lose him if he moved? "Are you going to take the tour?"

"I should. After that press conference, I don't know what will happen in the election next year."

"You have to believe the citizens of Cedar Corners are proud of the job you're doing."

"They might be today. Come election time, they might just remember my dad was a con who died in prison."

This seemed like a wonderful opportunity for him

yet she sensed he wasn't as enthusiastic about it as he should be. "Do you want to take the job?"

"I have to give it some thought."

The door seemed to bang shut on the discussion.

Maybe she'd hoped he'd say he didn't want to leave Cedar Corners because she was here. But they hadn't known each other very long and a few kisses were a far cry from any type of commitment. She didn't even know if she was ready to think about commitment.

As they ate, the warm breeze dried her skin and her bathing suit. It dried Simon's, too, but all that tanned taut skin was a monumental distraction. She had trouble keeping her mind on their conversation now that it had turned to more mundane matters.

"Have you heard from Janetta?" he asked, then tipped up a can of soda and took three long swallows.

She was mesmerized by the working of his throat muscles, his large hand on the can, the glistening moisture of his lips when he was finished drinking.

Combing her fingers through her hair to help dry it, warning herself Simon's job offer made anything between them even more precarious, she forked a strawberry from her cup of fruit salad. "She'll be home any day now. She couldn't tell me exactly when. I can't wait for her to meet Francie."

"She likes babies?"

"She says she wants a hoard of them some day, but she insists she might have to do it on her own."

"That could be a little tough."

The ironic humor in his tone made her smile. "She's prepared to adopt. She might even be thinking of older children who are hard to place. Janetta's always been the wild card in the family. We never know what she'll do."

"If she has to travel with her job, kids would be rough."

"She's up for a promotion. If she gets it, she'd supervise from Cedar Corners. I think she's waiting for that before she makes any decisions."

"What about you? You want more kids?"

"I'm going to concentrate on Francie for the time being."

Leaning closer, he ran his thumb down the side of her cheek. "Kids are a responsibility that never quits."

His touch unsettled her and made her shiver. "I don't think anyone knows how big a responsibility until they're a parent. I have to think of Francie first, foremost and always."

"Yes, you do. But you also have to think about yourself and what makes you happy. If you're not happy, *she* won't be."

"Happiness isn't like a butterfly you can catch with a net."

"No, but sometimes I think you're afraid to go after what makes you happy."

When she started to shake her head, he moved even closer.

Her breath caught. The look in his eyes was so deep and probing and tender, she had to be honest with him. "When I'm with you, I feel happy."

"What about when I kiss you?" His hands slid to her waist and then around her back. She could feel the imprint of each of his fingers. She could smell pine and grass and Simon. She could see banked desire in his eyes and she wondered what would happen if he let it free.

His lips were as hot as the molten sensation that seemed to invade her body when he kissed her. Freely she gave herself up to summer and the heat and every feminine need fighting to get free.

After her marriage to Todd, she'd felt so numb she didn't know if she'd ever feel again. She felt so much with Simon as his lips parted over hers, as his tongue played with hers, as her arms went around his sides. He was so hard and muscled and wonderfully male. Her hands stroked his back, and his groan said he liked it. Touching and being touched was as good as kissing. Her body was trying to absorb the sensations of his tongue plumbing her mouth, his taste of cola, his taste of Simon. At the same time, she was aware of his fingers skimming the edges of her swimsuit, coming very close to her breasts. Without even realizing what she was doing, her hands dipped to his waist and her fingers teased the edge of his swimsuit at his back.

His shudder rippled through her. She'd never felt so wild and wanton, so womanly, so intimately involved.

Birds chirped in the canopy of maples and redbuds. The sweet scents of late summer and pine were an intoxicating perfume. Simon's fervent, deep openmouthed kiss challenged her to let go and enjoy the pleasure between them, let go of her fears of what could come next.

When he broke the kiss to gaze into her eyes, the

passion there was so cogently primal that she whispered his name.

He must have taken that as a green light because he laid her down onto the blanket and stretched on top of her. Taking his weight on his arms, he kissed the soft sensitive skin along her jawline, tauntingly nipped her neck and teased down the strap on her shoulder. He was so hard against her, so consummately male.

Lost in a haze of desire, she ran her hands over his tight buttocks.

"Easy, Risa," he murmured. "I've only got so much control."

Control. She should stop this, she really should.

According to his reputation, Simon had had a lot of women. He might even be moving to Tulsa. On top of that, she didn't know if she could trust him not to change. What if he just wanted to woo her because he'd gone through all the women in Cedar Corners and she happened to be handy living next door? What if this didn't mean any more to him than a summer fling...something different...a way to pass days that had become too long?

She thought about Todd putting his fist through the wall.

Her body went rigid.

Apparently Simon felt the change because he raised his head, propped on his elbows, and asked, "What's wrong?"

She closed her eyes, expecting him to be angry, expecting him to blame her for all of this, expecting him to give up and go away. "Everything...everything is happening too fast. I shouldn't be doing this."

"Why not?" He didn't sound angry, but he did sound impatiently patient.

"Because I have a little girl to think about. I just started standing on my own two feet—" She stopped abruptly, not wanting to go into explanations about that.

However, Simon was an astute man and he'd gotten to know her pretty well in a short amount of time. She could see him bank the desire to a restrainable level. She could feel him move his body away from hers, so he was close but not too close.

"Tell me about your marriage," he said then, and it was more a demand than a request.

Instead of doing as he asked, she strove to sit up. Telling Simon about her marriage would be opening herself up to him completely, baring her heart and soul, confiding her weaknesses and fears. She couldn't do that yet. She simply didn't trust him enough.

"I don't want to discuss my marriage."

If he hadn't been angry before, there was a flicker of it now in his eyes as he pushed himself up and sat beside her. "You've said that before." He'd given her a bit of room but he still sat terrifically close.

His silence pushed her to add, "I can't. Not with you. Not yet."

His shoulders were squared and tense. "Not yet? Or not *ever?*"

She just didn't know. Yet she hesitatingly murmured, "Not yet."

Letting out a breath, he looked away from her into the trees. "Lucy told me Parker left you with debts…that your mother only saw what she wanted to see."

Her sister had a very big mouth sometimes, and that's why Risa hesitated to confide in her. "She shouldn't have told you anything. It's *my* business, not hers."

Simon's mouth tightened into a grim line, and his voice had a sharper edge to it as he asked, "You don't trust me, do you?"

"Trust takes time."

His response was quick and pointed. "No, I think trust takes action. You think about everything that's happened since I took you to the hospital that first time. You think about me catching your daughter in my hands. You think about kissing me and how I can make you forget the rest of the world."

"I don't even know if you're going to take that job in Tulsa!" she protested as if a job offer could make a difference, as if it might have something to do with trust.

"I don't know if I'm going to take it or not." He was frustrated now and it showed. "What's the real problem here, Risa?"

"I'm going to get dressed." She got to her feet.

Before she took a step, he stood, too, and clasped her arm. "You didn't answer me."

At that moment she felt trapped by what had happened in her marriage with Todd, by the decisions she'd chosen to make, by the attraction to Simon that couldn't be analyzed or wished away.

"The problem is, Sheriff Blackstone..." She needed to distance herself from him. "I just had a baby a month ago. I'm breast-feeding and my body's not back to normal yet. I don't know if I'm a diversion for you or the next woman in line from the list of available females in Cedar Corners. On top of all that, you expect me to make out with you as if I were a teenager on a Saturday night date. I was just getting my life back in order when you decided I needed your help. And because I won't tell you every minute detail of my life, you get all bent out of shape."

He didn't release his hold on her. "I don't want to know every minute detail of your life, just the important details, just the ones that I think affect what's happening between us."

"Stop pushing me, Simon."

"Stop running away from me, Risa."

Was that was she was doing? Running away from him? If she was running away from him, there was a very good reason. She was falling in love with him—a no-holds-barred, future-with-the-man kind of love.

The insight was so jolting, she pulled away. "I'm going to get dressed. I think you'd better take me home."

Tears came to her eyes as she hurried toward the clump of cedars and some privacy. She needed to absorb the knowledge that she loved Simon that much. She needed to sort out everything that had happened and everything that they'd said.

And then she needed to decide what she was going to do about all of it.

Chapter Nine

Simon dumped the remains of his frozen dinner into the garbage can. He knew he'd blown it. He'd pushed Risa further than he'd intended, and he wasn't exactly sure why. Her marriage *was* her business.

Still…

The fact that she didn't trust him pricked at him like a thistle that had somehow gotten into his boot.

Maybe she has reason not to trust men. Maybe she has reason not to trust you. Look at your track record.

He had no track record to speak of. That was the whole crux of the matter. Although he'd dated and bedded women since he was sixteen, with Risa he felt as if this were the first time for everything. He didn't like the feeling yet he *did* like Risa. Every time he was around her, his libido went wild, acting as if she were the hottest woman under the sun.

After that fiasco at the lake last week, she probably wanted to keep at least a mile between them.

He glanced out the window to see if there was any activity next door. He knew Janetta had come home yesterday…he'd seen her drive up in her silver sedan. Last evening he'd heard the women's laughter floating over from their porch. In the middle of the night last night, he'd wondered if Janetta was going to take the night feeding so that Risa could sleep.

None of that was any of his business.

Yet he felt as if all of it was his business.

On Saturday, as he'd supervised David and the other three troublemakers, he'd found satisfaction in watching them paint Mr. Truhenny's fence. He'd found satisfaction in the idea that he was helping them find the right path again. They'd been sweaty and tired and thirsty and hungry by the end of the morning. While they'd finished up, he'd bought fast food for them knowing they'd appreciate that most. And they'd eaten it in George Truhenny's kitchen while the older man told stories about a simpler life in Cedar Corners.

There was a city council meeting next week. That's when Simon would bring up the idea of the community center and getting some programs started for the kids of Cedar Corners.

When he opened his refrigerator, he saw the bottle of wine, the wedge of cheese and the box of strawberries that he'd purchased on his way home. Wishful thinking on his part. Yet if he could clear the air with Risa, assure her he could be patient as long as she needed him to be patient, maybe they could pop that cork and have a decent talk.

He remembered kissing her, touching her, and how she'd put a halt to it.

After he shut the refrigerator door hard, he went out the back door and crossed over the line into Janetta Lombardi's backyard. He rapped on the back door.

When Janetta came to the screened door, he was disappointed.

"Simon. Long time no see," she said with a grin.

He couldn't help but smile at her greeting. Janetta's hair was lighter brown than Francie's and much curlier. It was cut in a bubble style that made her face seem even rounder. She was taller than Risa and at least twenty pounds heavier.

He compared every woman he met these days with Risa.

"How was your trip?" he asked, not in the least bit interested in small talk, yet knowing it was the only way he'd get inside her house.

"Long, tiring, and remotely rewarding. I'm hoping I get a promotion out of it. Would you like to come in? Risa made oatmeal cookies this afternoon."

Stepping inside, he asked, "Is she busy?"

"You're here to see Risa?" she teased. "Here I thought you came over to welcome me home."

"Of course I did. But I also came over to see Risa."

"I heard what you did. Not only delivering Francie, but capturing those bank robbers. Risa wouldn't talk much about it, but Mama had a lot to say."

"I'll just bet she did."

At his wry tone, Janetta laughed. "I heard she managed to feed you a lot of her lasagna. I think she likes you. She mentioned she'd promised to make sausage bread for you the next time you came over."

He didn't know if there would be a next time. It all depended—

Everything inside of him went still when Risa walked into the kitchen.

"Hello, Simon," she said politely.

From the proud tilt of her chin, the rigid set of her spine, he knew this wasn't going to be easy. Trying to keep his tone even, he said to Janetta, "I'd like to talk to your sister privately."

"Here? Or at your place?" Janetta suggested.

"I'm not going anywhere," Risa said firmly. "I just got Francie to sleep. She might wake up again—"

"And she might not," Janetta cut in. "You've changed her, nursed her and put her to bed. Chances are good she'll sleep till ten o'clock like she did last night. Go on with Simon and take a break. I'll take care of her."

"She's *my* responsibility. Just because you're home now doesn't mean..."

Simon interrupted this time. "Janetta's sorry she missed the last few weeks. Let her spend some time with her niece."

"You're taking charge again," Risa murmured.

Crossing to her, he took her hand in his. "That's because we have to talk. Come over to the house with me."

When she didn't pull her hand away, he saw that as a good sign. When she didn't *look* away, he actually felt some hope. She was wearing a yellow checkered blouse and a pair of yellow shorts. She looked like sunshine, and that's exactly what she brought into his life.

"All right," she gave in. "Let me kiss Francie and then I'll go with you."

Simon suddenly realized Risa hadn't been inside his house before. A few minutes later as she glanced around at his bachelor residence, he wondered what she thought. There were vertical blinds at all of his windows but no drapes. He had a cleaning lady come in once a week but there were dishes stacked in the sink now, a police scanner on the counter, a pile of papers on the table.

Not commenting on any of it, Risa followed him into his living room.

He'd bought the living room furniture on sale when he'd bought the house. There was a denim-covered couch, a suede-like recliner, a bulky pine coffee table and entertainment center. A collection of antique sheriffs' badges in a display case hung above the sofa, and a print of a gray wolf decorated another wall. He'd found the huge Navajo patterned rug at a flea market. Its reds, rusts, greens and blues livened the whole room.

"This is nice," Risa said appreciatively.

"You like it?" Janetta's house was decorated in all flowers and peach and cream. He thought that might be Risa's taste, too.

"I like it a lot. It's comfortable and casual."

He motioned toward the sofa. "Would you like something to drink?"

"No, I'm fine."

He wasn't sure she wanted to be there because she perched on the edge of the sofa as if ready to make a hasty exit.

Sitting beside her, his jean-clad leg brushed her bare one. When she turned toward him, he saw the uncertainty in her eyes.

Taking his cell phone from his belt, he set it on the coffee table. "There's something I need to tell you," he said soberly, holding her gaze with his. "Ever since you moved in with Janetta in January, I haven't dated. I haven't wanted to date—not anyone but you."

Her brown eyes grew huge with his confession. "But we hardly ever spoke. You didn't *know* me."

"That's the thing, Risa. I felt I did. Not in any complete sense. But I saw you coming and going. I heard you talking with Janetta in the yard. I was attracted to you more than I've been attracted to any woman I've ever dated."

"But my pregnancy started showing."

"Yes, it did. Damn if that didn't intrigue me, too. And those times when we did say hello or talk about the weather, I didn't feel my interest was one-sided. Was it?"

It was a moment before she answered him. "No, it wasn't. I noticed you, too. I'm not sure when. I was confused when I first moved in with Janetta. But you were always kind and when we talked..."

She blushed but she didn't stop. "I felt breathless and excited and wouldn't admit it to myself. It wasn't until you swept me up into your arms that day on the porch that I realized my tummy doing somersaults had nothing to do with the pregnancy."

There was no guile in Risa and that was one of the reasons he was so drawn to her. Sliding his hand up her neck, his fingers laced in her hair.

"Come here," he whispered.

She tipped her face up to his, and he'd never wanted her more. When his lips covered hers, he tried to hold back. But the desire he felt was screaming too loudly for him to squelch it. As his tongue mated with hers, the kiss went on and on and on until he broke it off so that they could both come up for air.

Needing to grab onto his control once more, he gathered her close and just held her.

Her cheek was against his shoulder, her hand on his chest when she said, "I can feel your heart."

"It's a little wound up right now," he admitted with a wry smile.

Risa tilted her head up and studied him so closely he wondered what she was looking for.

"I told you I was confused when I moved in with Janetta."

His heart continued to pound hard but now it was for a different reason. "Confused about what?"

She pushed away from him and sat up straighter. "You know who Todd was. You know the good reputation he had."

Simon nodded. Todd Parker's career as a neurologist and his philanthropy had been splashed over the *Cedar Corners Examiner* when the doctor had become chief of staff...and after he died.

"I met him when I consulted with him about one of my students," she went on, looking down at her hands in her lap. "Besides her reading problem, she had physical symptoms that led the nurse to recommend an appointment with a neurologist. Her family chose Todd.

He was very gracious with me, very charming, very caring when we discussed her. After our meeting, he asked me to have dinner with him."

When she stopped, Simon waited. He knew she had to tell this in her own way...in her own time.

"You've met my family. You know that what you see is what you get. That's what I grew up with. That's the way it's always been. I suppose I was naive, but I thought everyone was like that. I didn't date much in college. I was concerned with my studies, making the dean's list, going on for my master's. Besides that, my faith as well as my background convinced me I wanted to be a virgin on my wedding night. I was waiting for the right man...the perfect man. Todd seemed to be that. My family, especially my mother, thought he walked on water. It wasn't until after we were married that I realized the real Todd Parker was very different from the man who had charmed me."

"Tell me about it," Simon urged her.

Shifting on the sofa cushion, she moved a little farther away from him. "Todd became critical, making comments about what I did and how I did it. He complained about the meals I made, made remarks about how he disliked the clothes I wore, questioned how much time I spent with the work I brought home at night. I didn't realize what was happening, but little by little he was eroding my self-confidence."

When she paused, Simon found his tension increased. He suspected this story wouldn't be pretty.

"Todd became more demanding about what he wanted...in our home...in our bed. He convinced me to stop teaching and to support him in his bid for chief of staff by making friends with other doctors' wives, by joining organizations, by playing bridge with Cedar Corners' society matrons. One day, I came home from one of those bridge sessions, sat on the sofa in our beautifully furnished but very empty house and wondered what my life had become. I questioned whatever I did. In fact, I let Todd tell me what to do. It seemed the best way to keep peace. A few weeks after that, the reading specialist that had taken my place at the elementary school resigned to move with her husband to Arkansas. One of the teachers called me to tell me about it. I knew I wanted back in. I knew I wanted to do worthwhile work. I knew I had to analyze my life and my marriage and figure out how to make it work."

"Did you talk to Parker about any of this?"

Still Risa didn't meet his gaze. "I tried, but he didn't want to hear it. He walked away when something didn't suit him. But he couldn't walk away from the fact that I told him I was going back to teaching. That's when I first saw the anger."

Simon went perfectly still. "What do you mean?"

"I tried to have a discussion with Todd, but he ended up shouting at me, warning me that no wife of his was going to embarrass him by working as a schoolteacher. He stormed out that night and didn't come back home. I worried, called the hospital, checked with the highway patrol. But Todd was fine. He'd driven to Oklahoma City, spent the night there in a bar and taken a hotel room. At the time, I wondered if he'd taken another woman to bed, but I convinced myself not to think the worst of him. When he did come home the following night, he was still angry. He didn't talk to me for a week—a solid week. No one had ever given me the silent treatment before, but I finally saw it for what it was—a means of control. I told him he could be silent from now until the turn of the next century but I was going back to teaching."

"He finally accepted it?"

Now her chin came up and she looked at him. "He accepted it, but didn't like it and took every opportunity to point out how it interfered with our lives. We became more and more distant. His criticism was constant. I went to see a counselor and realized my background had set me up for a relationship with Todd. Mama always believed she should wait on my dad hand-and-foot and that's what he wanted from her. She never questioned him. She never contradicted him. That's what I saw in their marriage."

"So you fell into the same pattern with your husband?" Simon asked.

"For a while—before I woke up and saw what I was becoming. That's one of the reasons I went back to work. After a week of silence, I thought he'd accepted it. School started, but I made sure I still had dinners ready for him. He often worked late, so it was no problem getting my work done. But then we had a program at school. Todd knew that's where I'd be. But after the program my car wouldn't start and another teacher—a male teacher—brought me home. It was pouring down rain, and he walked me to the door with his umbrella. Todd opened the door and his expression—"

She shook her head. "I just can't describe it. It was a mixture of jealousy and possessiveness and anger. I felt fear when Mark left and I told myself that was silly. But it wasn't so silly. Todd yelled that he didn't want me near that other man. He shouted that he wanted to know where I was every minute. He told me the next time I had a program at school, he'd take me and bring me home."

"How did you react?"

"I didn't know what to do. I had taken vows. I had always been committed to my marriage. But I was beginning to fear Todd and I knew we needed counseling. That night he left and stayed out till three in the morning. When he returned, he slept in the guest room."

"Thank God," Simon muttered.

"He never hurt me, Simon, in fact—" She glanced away but then met his gaze squarely. "You're going to think I'm an idiot and foolish and the weakest woman you've ever known, but you wanted to know the truth and here it is. The next night, Todd came home with flowers and an apology. He said he'd had a rough day and the stress had gotten out of hand. Financial difficulties the hospital was having were weighing on him, and I believed that. But I also knew we needed counseling and I told him so."

She rushed on now, in a hurry to get the story over with. "He...kissed me. He told me we didn't need a counselor, we needed a vacation in Barbados. He would make the reservations and we'd go over Thanksgiving. I tried to protest but he was so gentle, so tender with me and I didn't want to give up on our marriage, not if

I didn't have to. My vows meant everything. We…we made love that night."

Although Simon's heart was pounding in his ears, he took a deep breath and told himself he had to listen. He had to understand.

"But afterward, Todd told me he had a present for me. He gave me a cell phone. He told me he wanted me to carry it with me always so he could get hold of me anytime he wanted to. That's when I knew nothing had changed. We needed that counselor and when I said so, this time he got angry again. But I wasn't going to back down. When I didn't, he got so mad, he punched his fist right through the wall. He scared me so badly, I couldn't stop shaking. I think it shocked some sense into him. It also shocked sense into me. I told him we should separate for a while. If he wanted to go to counseling, I would do that with him. But until he made a decision, I would be living with Janetta."

October first. Simon remembered that night and the accident he'd been called to at one in the morning.

"You went to Janetta's?"

"Yes. Todd locked himself in his den and I packed. I tried to talk to him again before I left, but he wouldn't answer me. I didn't want to go, but I knew I couldn't stay. When I showed up on Janetta's doorstep, she didn't ask any questions."

Risa's voice became thready and emotion filled her eyes. "It was almost two when we got the call. The hospital couldn't reach me at the house. A nurse there remembered my family and called my mother and then they called Janetta's. It was raining heavily when I left.

But I guess later the streets became flooded and Todd was going too fast—"

Her voice broke and all Simon could do was take her into his arms and hold her tight. Then he kissed her and she kissed him back. The past faded away and only now mattered.

As his tongue stroked hers, he caressed her face, let loose his control on his desire, and revelled in the feel of her hardening nipples against his chest. The earth was definitely shaking and he knew there was going to be upheaval in his life like he'd never seen before. At the moment, he didn't care. All he cared about was taking more pleasure with Risa, giving her more pleasure in return. They could be intimate without actually—

His cell phone rang from where he'd placed it on the coffee table before they'd started kissing. He thought about letting it ring, but the insistent beep reminded him of his duty, and he regretfully broke away from Risa.

"Let me check the caller ID," he murmured. "If it's not important, I won't take it."

But it *was* important. It was Anson Foster, one of the deputies. Giving Risa a last fast kiss, he leaned forward on the sofa and pressed enter. "What's up, Anson?"

"Nothing good. I've got some kids here and knew you'd want to know about this, especially since one of them is Risa Parker's nephew."

The heat suddenly went out of Simon's blood. "Tell me."

As Simon listened, anger replaced desire—anger at himself, thinking he could put four boys on the straight and narrow, anger at David for doing something so foolish, anger at David's parents for not keeping a closer watch on their son, for being too lenient.

When Anson finished, Simon assured him, "I'll be there as soon as I can." He ended the call and turned to face Risa. "David is down at the sheriff's office."

"The sheriff's office?" She was totally baffled.

He wished this was the first time *he* was hearing about David and his problems. "David has been running with some older boys. Tonight in a convenience store parking lot, the oldest boy with David tried to hot-wire a car. I feel partly responsible."

Risa's eyes were huge. "I don't understand. Hot-wire a car? As in *steal* it?"

"Probably more like take it for a joyride. Apparently it belonged to an older friend of Joey Martin's. That's one of the boys David's been running with."

"How do you know that? Why do *you* feel partly responsible?"

"This isn't the sheriff's department's first encounter with David. Remember those vandals I told you about who painted the water tower and the road signs?"

"Yes, in fact, you were called away—"

"Last week we finally had a witness who saw the kids deface a road sign. Mr. Truhenny knew Joey and could describe the others, including their bikes. I went to the school, pulled them out of class and confronted them. One of the boys was David. They were all repentant, and David pleaded with me not to tell his parents."

The blood drained from Risa's face.

Simon went on anyway. "I thought they just had too

much time on their hands and needed something constructive to do. On Saturday I supervised them painting Mr. Truhenny's picket fence. It took most of the morning and they seemed to understand the consequences of bad behavior. But apparently the thrill of trying something new held more allure for them."

Now Risa moved a good six inches away from Simon and color came back into her face. "Why didn't you tell me?"

"I couldn't tell you. I'd made a pact with David. I was hoping a morning painting the fence would teach him his lesson and that would be the end of it."

All of a sudden she was looking at him as if she didn't know him. "I can't believe you didn't tell me or Dom or Lucy. If David had gotten into that car with a twelve-year-old driving, they could have been in an accident and hurt! That would have been *your* fault."

"In part it would have been my fault. I made a mistake in judgment," he admitted gruffly.

"It was *more* than a mistake in judgment, Simon. Not only did you put David in jeopardy, but you betrayed my trust. I just poured my heart and soul out to you. I told you things I haven't told another living soul, not even Janetta. You asked me to trust you, and I did."

"Risa, David has nothing to do with us."

"David has *everything* to do with us. You kept information that concerns my family from me."

"You're overreacting," he said impatiently now, seeing the guardedness come back into her eyes, feeling the distance she was putting between them again.

"Overreacting." She shook her head. "That's the

same phrase Todd always used when I didn't agree with him, or I didn't go along with what he wanted…when I had feelings of my own."

Maybe Risa was upset, but her comparison stung. "I'm nothing like your dead husband. If you can't see that, then we have no place to go from here."

"We *don't* have anyplace to go from here," she agreed, standing now. "Did your deputy call Dom and Lucy?"

Could she cut everything off between them so easily in her concern for her family? Apparently so.

Standing, too, he hooked the phone onto his belt. "Yes. Your sister and brother-in-law are on the way to the station."

Risa would have turned and left, but he caught her arm. "I'll drive you."

Yanking away from his grasp, she said defiantly, "I'll drive myself."

Chapter Ten

The sheriff's office was sheer bedlam as Risa stepped inside. With Janetta watching a sleeping Francie, Risa felt she had to be there as a support for Dom and Lucy. They were standing beside her mother who was seated on the hard wooden bench. Parents of the other boys were conferring nearby.

Instinctively Risa's gaze went to Simon who had obviously arrived before her. His expression was grim as he spoke to Anson Foster in the hallway leading to the interview rooms. As Risa made her way to Dom and Lucy, Simon glanced at her, his expression not changing.

She looked away, feeling more betrayed than ever.

She'd trusted him, she'd almost let him—

Her heart ached because he hadn't told her about David and the vandalism.

She'd just given Lucy a comforting hug and learned

one of her sister's neighbors was watching Tanya and Mary Lou when Simon's voice filled the room. "Listen up, everyone."

The whole group came to attention at the authority in his voice. Risa wasn't surprised at that but right now she resented it.

"The boys are with Deputy Garrity in interview room one. He's not interrogating them, he's just baby-sitting them. I'd like all of the parents to join me in room two. I'm going to let you know what the witnesses at the convenience store told us, what direction we need to take with these boys before they get into more serious trouble. Then I want to meet with each boy and each set of parents separately. That's the plan. Anyone have any objections?"

The room went quiet until Dom asked, "Do I need to call a lawyer?"

The sharp edge in Simon's tone lessened. "Let's conference first, then you can decide."

That seemed to satisfy the group and moments later, parents were following Simon into one of the rooms.

"I guess I can't go in there with them," Carmen complained.

Risa heard the door shut firmly on the closed session. "No, we'll have to wait here."

"I can't believe David would do such a thing! He's a good boy. Maybe all of this is some kind of mistake."

Lowering herself to the bench beside her mother, Risa said, "It's no mistake. David was in trouble before this and we just didn't know it."

"What do you mean, he was in trouble?"

Risa related everything Simon had told her. When she was finished, Carmen looked at her curiously. "How do you know all this?"

"Simon told me."

"When?"

"Tonight. After he got the phone call about the boys trying to hot-wire the car." Her voice must have indicated her hurt and turmoil because her mother's expression softened.

"What's wrong?" Carmen asked.

"What's wrong? Simon didn't think I needed to know what was happening with David. If he had told us, tonight never would have happened."

"You don't know that."

The last thing Risa expected was for her mother to defend Simon. "I *do* know that. Dom and Lucy would have done something."

"What would they have done? Ordered David to his room with his computer and television and anything he could ever want? How would that have kept tonight from happening?"

Would Dom and Lucy have cracked down on David for the vandalism? Or would they have looked the other way, adhering to the "boys will be boys" philosophy?

"It looks to me like Simon tried to teach them responsibility," her mother commented.

"He could have told me and still have taught them responsibility. I trusted him. I thought we had something special, and he kept this from me as if I were just...anyone." The sense of betrayal was still so strong, she was much too close to tears.

Her mother went quiet after Risa's outburst. There was a sympathetic look in her eyes every time Risa glanced at her which led Risa to believe Carmen might suspect what was going on inside of her.

The waiting seemed interminable. Dom and Lucy joined Risa and her mother after the parent-sheriff session was over. Joey and his parents were first to conference with Simon and when they'd finished, the boy and his parents left the building looking seriously upset.

"They're in real trouble," Lucy said with tears in her eyes. "This will go on David's record."

Dom clasped his wife's shoulder. "Hold on now. Let's just see what Simon has to say when he meets with us." He glanced at Risa. "He just gave us the facts in there, who the witnesses were and what they saw."

"Did he tell you about the vandalism?" Risa asked.

As Lucy swiped a tear from her cheek, she replied, "Yes, and he said he made an error in judgment in not contacting us before. He thought earning their confidence and teaching them a lesson was all they needed."

Simon had been wrong, just as she had been wrong about *him*.

Fifteen minutes later, David was reunited with his parents for their conference with Simon. His face was pale and there were tear streaks down his cheeks.

"I think he's sorry," Carmen whispered to Risa. "That's a good sign."

Risa didn't know if David was sorry, but, yes, he was scared. She was sure of that a short time later when Lucy, Dom and David emerged from the hallway.

Lucy's face was drawn as she crossed to Risa and Carmen. "We have to meet with the judge at the courthouse tomorrow morning. He'll determine David's punishment. Simon thinks that's necessary to drive home the seriousness of what they did."

Dom came up behind her. "As much as I hate putting David through this, I know Simon's right. We don't want anything like this ever happening again. There are going to have to be changes." He glanced over at his son who was waiting for them by the door. "Let's take him home and talk about rules. Maybe we can figure out how to put him on the right path again."

Lucy gave Risa a hug. "Thanks for being here. I know it helped Mama for you to be here. She insisted on coming along."

When Risa leaned away, she gazed at her sister. "Of course she did. That's Mama."

The two sisters exchanged weak smiles, though the last thing Risa felt like doing was smiling. She looked over Lucy's shoulder and caught Simon's gaze. There was no tenderness or gentleness there. There was only the iron look of a man who was doing his job.

Turning to her sister, knowing she and Simon had nothing to say to each other, Risa suggested, "Let's go home."

Gray clouds gathered again in the midday sky on Thursday afternoon. Risa was taking comfort in feeding her daughter. But even Francie's little body so close to hers made her think of Simon, the day he'd delivered her daughter, the way he held her. Risa's heart and soul felt as if they'd been turned inside out and upside down.

Yesterday she'd waited outside the judge's chambers with Francie and her mother as David, Dom and Lucy went inside. They'd been in there a half hour. When they'd come out, Dom's face had been strained. Lucy had had tear tracks running down her cheeks and David had looked pale and shaken. The judge had been stern, with no intention of letting David off lightly. Yet he'd taken Sheriff Simon Blackstone's recommendations.

Every Saturday with the three other boys and under Simon's supervision, the four of them would help elderly residents of the town with jobs, repairs and yard work. In addition, the judge had decreed the boys would spend four hours a week working for a volunteer organization. The judge had shown David a list of possibilities and David had chosen the animal shelter. All of this would continue for the next six months and during that time David would report to Simon once a week with a log of his activities. Dom and Lucy were also to enforce a curfew. If David broke it, he would be back before the judge.

Risa had learned from Lucy the other three boys would be reporting to two other deputies rather than Simon. She had been thinking about that a lot ever since her sister had told her about it.

Thunder rumbled outside as the tree branches swayed in a suddenly stronger wind.

Risa had just laid a sleeping Francie in the bassinet that would soon be too small, when she heard a pounding on the back door. Seconds later, Simon called, "Risa, are you in there?"

Her heart sped up as tears came to her eyes. A flood

of memories washed over her—tender moments, exasperating moments...intimate moments.

Hurrying to the kitchen, she opened the door and saw he was wearing his uniform. This definitely was an official visit.

"I'm here," she said, going breathless. She looked up into his dark eyes.

"Where's Francie?" he asked with an edge to his voice.

"Sleeping in the living room."

"Get her and go to the storm cellar. Now."

"Why? I—"

"Tornado warning. One touched down on the other side of Union City. Come on."

"I hate the idea of taking her into a dark, damp place..."

Simon stepped inside. He was big and sweaty and looked to be at the end of his tether. "Dark and damp is better than a house in smithereens all around both of you." He went to her refrigerator and removed two bottles of water. "What else do you need besides diapers?" he asked, opening her pantry closet where he knew she kept extras.

As he grabbed a few, he barked, "What else?"

His urgency was alarming her. "Conditions are that serious?"

"Look at the sky!"

She'd been so lost in her thoughts, so intent on feeding her baby, that she hadn't noticed what was happening around her. The sky was indeed gray with a greenish tint. There were huge, low-slung, billowing clouds that looked as if they were dropping lower every second. Simon wasn't trying to scare her, he was doing his job. He had a lot of other people to take care of, too.

"There are some supplies already in the storm cellar—a battery-operated radio and flashlights. Janetta just changed all the batteries in the spring. I'll get Francie."

He looked relieved she finally saw the danger in the situation. When she searched for more than relief on his face, she couldn't find it. She'd ended it between them. She'd told him he'd broken their trust. As far as he was concerned, it was over. It was over for her, too, wasn't it?

That thought was too painful. Spinning around, she raced for the living room. Instead of just scooping up her daughter, she scooped up the mattress under her as well as the blanket in the bassinet. Risa kept it there for when the air-conditioning was on. Now she was glad Francie was still so small and didn't know exactly what was going on. Risa knew she had to stay calm or her daughter would feel her fear.

Leaning down, she put her lips to Francie's forehead. "It'll be all right, baby. We'll be just fine. We're just going to a safe place for a little while."

Returning to the kitchen, she saw Simon was already heading out the door.

The wind was almost howling now, branches whipping this way and that. The air was clammy, filled with moisture and she almost felt as if she were in a steam bath.

Simon's Stetson suddenly swirled from his head and

he uttered a curse. But he didn't go after it. He concentrated on unlatching the heavy storm cellar door and lifting it open one-handed as he clutched the water and diapers in his other arm.

"Get down there," he yelled. "Now!"

Risa was protecting Francie with her body as leaves, twigs and then somebody's roof shingle sailed across the yard. Simon's shirt billowed at his back and he looked as if he were the only sturdy, stable ballast in the world that wouldn't blow away. He wasn't in her life now. He was just making sure she and Francie were safe. The wind pushed against Risa and she fought it as she hurried into the storm cellar.

Going down the steps quickly, she laid Francie on the mattress in the black cavern and picked up a flashlight. When she switched it on, the bright beam was reassuring.

Simon leapt down the steps, deposited the water and diapers beside Francie, then turned to go.

"You should stay here, Simon."

"You know I can't. I have to go back out into it. That's my job."

His job was his life. Nothing was more important to him than that.

The phone on Simon's belt beeped. At the same time, Risa heard a woman's voice call her name. It was Janetta.

Climbing up the steps, she called, "I'm here."

Her sister raced from the back porch down the concrete steps. "I was worried when I couldn't find you and Francie. At work I heard that two tornadoes had touched down."

"Three," Simon said grimly after he ended his phone conversation. "I've got to go." To both of them, he said, "Don't even think about opening the doors until you hear it's all clear on the radio or someone I authorize comes to get you."

With a last look at Risa that made her breath hitch, he hurried up the stairs and closed the storm cellar door. Janetta fumbled with the latch, hooking it behind him.

Tears came to Risa's eyes as she gathered her daughter up into her arms. That was when the realization struck her that she might never see Simon again. He was in danger! He was going out into that storm as if he thought he was impervious to it. She couldn't let him do that. She loved him. She wasn't just *falling* in love with him...she was way beyond the fall.

She loved him.

Tears fell more freely now, and she put Francie in Janetta's arms. "I have to go after him. I have to tell him I love him. If something happens to him, he'll never know. He'll think I'm still—"

Janetta caught Risa's arm in a firm grip and wouldn't let loose. "You're not going anywhere. You can't. You have to think of your own welfare and Francie's. What's she going to do if you get hurt? Simon is strong and capable. He'll be fine."

"But what if something happens to him? What if he never knows how I feel? I thought...I felt betrayed. I still can't understand why he didn't tell me about David. I love him so much."

Janetta motioned to the floor. "Come on. Let's sit."

With a last glance at the door, Risa knew Janetta was right. Simon was capable and strong and smart. She had to trust that he wouldn't purposely put himself in harm's way.

Trust. What a complicated word.

When Risa took Francie and settled her on her lap, Janetta pulled a power bar from her pants pocket, broke it in half and gave half to Risa.

After Janetta took a bite and munched for a few moments, she swallowed. "There *are* two sides to this situation. The way I see it, David is the one who did something wrong, not Simon."

"But David wouldn't have been caught with those boys yesterday if Simon would have told me about it," Risa protested.

"What would *you* have done?"

"I would have sat down with Dom and Lucy."

"And what would *they* have done?"

That was the same question her mother had asked. Risa brushed Francie's fine hair over her brow, knowing exactly what Janetta was getting at...the same point her mother had made. "You don't think they would have done anything."

"I don't think they would have. They might have scolded David and told him not to do it again. After being around Dom and Lucy, I think Simon knew that."

"So he took matters into his own hands and look what happened."

Janetta nudged Risa's arm with hers. "Stop being hurt for a moment and look at this from *his* perspective. He's a law-and-order kind of guy. These kids veered away from the straight and narrow. If he had told their parents, they would have seen him as just an uncaring authority figure. Instead, he tried to gain their confidence. My guess is they didn't want their parents to know. He worked with that. He thought if he taught them the consequences of their behavior, they wouldn't step out of line again. Okay, he was wrong. But it was an error in judgment. He didn't set out to betray you. He didn't set out to lie to you. And he didn't. Confidentiality is part of his job. Once he made the promise to those boys not to tell, how could he? This isn't black and white, Risa. Simon isn't Todd. If you love him as you say you do, you're going to have to accept the fact that even though he's the sexiest hunk alive, he's still human. He's going to make mistakes, just as you're going to make mistakes."

She thought about everything Janetta had said for a long time. "He pushed a hot button," she muttered, "when he told me I overreacted."

"*Did* you overreact?"

Wasn't *that* the million dollar question? She could blame it on hormones. She could blame it on her marriage to Todd. But she wouldn't be honest with herself if she did that. She'd overreacted because she'd been afraid. She'd been afraid to trust Simon's feelings for her. She'd been afraid to trust her feelings for him.

She wasn't afraid of them now. She wanted to tell him all about them. She wanted to tell him she was sorry for not believing in him…for not believing they could have a future together.

He hadn't betrayed her. He'd been trying to protect all of them—David, her, Dom and Lucy, her mother. Maybe it had been a mistake in judgment, and she wasn't even sure of that anymore. But it *hadn't* been a betrayal. She had overreacted this time because she was so afraid of loving Simon. If she hadn't let fear cloud her judgment, she would have realized that.

The only sound in the cellar was the crunch of Janetta's teeth on the rest of the power bar. Taking one of the bottles, she opened it, drank a few swallows of water and capped the bottle again.

"What are you thinking about?" her sister asked.

Before Risa could respond, something heavy and large hit the door of the storm cellar. Then they heard the wind howl until it was almost a roar. Risa took Janetta's hand and they said a prayer together, praying that Cedar Corners would be spared and no lives lost.

The noise stopped and an eerie silence took its place. Risa leaned low over her daughter and kissed her cheek. Even in the shadows, Risa could see her daughter looking up at her with all the trust and innocence of any child. Risa's heart overflowed with her love for Francie and her family...and for Simon.

When Janetta switched on the radio, through the static they learned another tornado had indeed touched down, felled some power lines, demolished a few parked cars and a lot of fence at a nearby farm. The damage was still being assessed. They listened to the drone of the announcer's voice until Francie fell asleep on Risa's lap. A half hour later, they learned it was safe to leave the storm cellar.

After Janetta opened the door, she carried Francie up into a much brighter day. One of the maples in Simon's yard lay uprooted across the hedge. Tree branches, a few lawn chairs, and the top of the bird bath were scattered across their yard. But other than that, everything else looked to be intact.

The two women went inside the house, half expecting pictures to be slanted on the walls and windows broken. But nothing was out of place or damaged and the power was still on.

"We were so lucky," Risa breathed, holding her daughter close.

"Yes, we were."

But where was Simon? Was he unharmed? Or had he somehow been right in the path of the tornado?

She had to know. She had to find him. She had to tell him she loved him.

Janetta was putting the mattress back in Francie's bassinet.

"I need a favor," Risa said.

"Anything. We just survived a tornado together."

Yes, they had. Risa never should have let Simon go out into it without telling him how she felt, without trying to work everything out. He obviously thought she'd written him off. He obviously thought everything was over between them. She'd believed it was, too, but she'd been wrong.

Hoping it wasn't too late, hoping she could mend the tear she'd caused, she asked Janetta, "Will you watch Francie? I have to go find Simon."

"It's a mess out there," Janetta said with some surprise. "Trees are probably down. Power lines are down. How far do you think you're going to get?"

"As far as Simon. I have to see him."

Janetta studied her for several moments. Seeing her sister's resolution and her determination, she picked up the phone to check it. "We've got a dial tone." Then she went to her purse which she'd dropped on the sofa and dug inside for her cell phone.

Handing it to Risa, she ordered, "If you get stuck, let me know. I don't want to sit here worrying all the time you're gone."

Risa took the cell phone and Janetta gathered Francie into her arms. "My niece and I will spend some quality time together. Don't rush back, just let me know you're okay."

After Risa managed to hug Janetta and Francie both, she grabbed her purse from the kitchen counter and hurried over to Simon's house. The back door was open. There was only one way she could find out where he was—by listening to his scanner. She suspected she'd find him where the most damage had occurred. If she got into the thick of it and found one of his deputies, he could direct her to Simon.

It only took her a few minutes to figure out most of Cedar Corners' law enforcement had gathered near the Murphys' farm at the north end of town. As Risa drove, she saw great swaths of destruction intermittently scattered on what was otherwise a peaceful landscape. The center of town seemed to have escaped unscathed except for debris from trees, in the street and along the lawns, a split-rail fence toppled over and a door ripped from a tractor shed. In the area hit the hardest, she spotted a large satellite dish collapsed onto a lawn and trees snapped in two.

As she approached the Murphys' farm, she could see the farmhouse had lost half its roof and the front windows were shattered. Simon's SUV and a cruiser were parked zigzag across the lane. Bystanders with nothing better to do had already gathered on the other side of the road. She had to find a deputy who knew her so law enforcement didn't think she was just another curious bystander. Yellow tape and orange cones marked the area around a downed telephone pole.

Parking well away from that, she ran to the entrance of the long driveway where she saw Deputy Garrity. He was standing by the side of his car and talking on his radio.

"An F2? A hundred and twenty miles an hour? We're lucky we didn't have more damage. No lives lost that we heard. The twister even missed the herd of cows on the Murphy place."

Deputy Garrity must have sensed Risa's approach. Turning, his eyes widened as he recognized her. Holding up his index finger, indicating he'd be finished soon, he ended the conversation and clicked off the radio.

"What are you doing here?" he asked curiously.

"I need to speak to Simon. It's important."

"We aren't letting any civilians on the scene until we check it out more thoroughly. The Murphys have gone into town to stay with relatives."

"I promise I won't touch anything or walk anywhere I shouldn't. I need to talk to Simon. Please."

The deputy must have seen something in her eyes,

something in the expression on her face. He pointed to the farmhouse. "Over there, along the right side, talking to the lineman from the power company. *Don't* tell him *I* let you through."

Before the deputy could change his mind or bar her from the site altogether, she headed down the long driveway, stopping for a second, her gaze searching for the white power truck and finding it.

Simon was engaged in a conversation with the lineman.

With no plan in mind, no thought except getting to him, she ran to his side.

"What are you doing here?" he asked gruffly. "You shouldn't be anywhere near the area. Something wrong? Did something happen to Francie?"

His first thought was for her daughter and she loved him for that, too. "No, Francie's fine. She's with Janetta. I know you have important work to do. But I have to talk to you."

Simon glanced at the lineman who was studying them both curiously. "Go home, Risa. We can talk tonight."

"No," she replied firmly. "I have to tell you something *now.*"

"What?" he demanded, obviously frustrated and exasperated with her.

Since he wasn't going to be cooperative, since she simply had no choice, she looked up into his smoky blue eyes and said what she had to say. "I love you, Simon. I'm sorry I overreacted Tuesday night. I know you didn't mean to hurt me and you were doing what you thought was best. I never should have said what I did. I never—"

With a dark flush staining his cheeks, Simon cast a glance at the amused lineman, took Risa's arm and ushered her to a debris-free space near the house, a good twenty feet from where the lineman stood.

She'd never seen him look more serious as he said, "You had every right to feel whatever you felt. But if you felt betrayed, then you don't know me."

She would have jumped in, but he shook his head to stop her and went on. "There are times when I have to keep aspects of my work confidential. This was one of them. What would happen if I couldn't tell you about a case I was working on?"

At his expression and the tone of his voice, her heart sank until she finally absorbed his words. *What would happen?* he'd asked. That meant he was thinking in terms of the future.

She was suddenly filled with hope. "I'll understand," she said with complete certainty. "If I don't, we'll discuss it until I *do* understand. Simon, I've never been more sure about anything than I am about my love for you and my faith in the kind of man you are. You're brave and protective and gentle and I'll trust you with my life and Francie's if you decide that's what you want."

After a long searching look that seemed to penetrate not only her heart but her soul, the shadows left his eyes, and the defenses he'd surrounded himself with since Tuesday night came tumbling down.

Clasping her shoulders with both of his hands, he declared, "I want *you*."

Her heart was racing so fast she couldn't speak.

He must have seen that as he went on. "I've thought of Francie as mine ever since I held her when she was born. I was going to give you a few days to think about what happened. Then I was going to court you like crazy. I was *not* going to let you get away. I love you, Risa. I'm going to stay in Cedar Corners, win the next election and be the best lawman I know how to be. Will you marry me?"

There were no doubts in Risa's heart. Simon was her soulmate.

"Yes," she managed. Her arms went around his neck as he enfolded her close to his body.

His kiss was long and deep and hungry, sweeping her away.

Reluctantly, he tore his lips from hers and murmured into her neck, "I think we have an audience."

Looking over his shoulder, she saw his lawman's instincts were indeed correct. Not only was the lineman standing there with a huge grin, but two deputies were, too.

When Simon turned to face them with Risa in his arms, she gave them a thumbs-up sign.

"Don't you men have work to do?" Simon asked with a mock scowl.

Their smiles widened. "Sure do, Sheriff," Anson answered. "I figure you have another five minutes before a crowd gathers to watch their sheriff kissing his girl. You know how fast rumors travel. But we'll see if we can't move them in another direction until you're done here."

As they walked away, chuckling among themselves, Simon pulled Risa close again. "I'll never be done here."

Then he kissed her with the intensity of a man who intended to love her for a lifetime.

Epilogue

"Will you play ball with me?" David asked Simon as Risa helped Carmen clear the Sunday dinner table.

Janetta, Dom and Lucy had gone into the living room with the girls. Tanya was getting dressed in her Christmas costume. She wanted to give her grandmother a preview of the performance she'd be giving on Wednesday night.

"It's cold out there," Carmen said to her grandson. She looked out the kitchen window. The trees were bare now with only two weeks until Christmas. The temperature had been holding in the forties.

Simon, who was cradling Francie in his arms, gave a shrug. "It's probably never too cold to toss a football."

Every time Risa gazed at Simon and their daughter, her heart was so full it felt as if it would burst. Simon was a wonderful father and a wonderful husband. In the two months since they'd been married, she'd given thanks every day that he'd charged into her life. He'd even made a difference in David's life. The two of them were pals now and spent a lot of time together. Throughout David's community service they had formed a genuine friendship.

"I suppose if you bundle up," Carmen mused, referring to football and this weather.

"I'll bundle up," Simon assured her and gave David a wink.

Simon kissed Risa and then she held out her arms for her baby. After he settled Francie in her arms, he whispered close to her ear, "I have a surprise for you when we get home."

"You're not going to tell me what it is?"

"It wouldn't be a surprise if I did." Then he gave her a quick but thorough kiss, waited for David to zip up his parka and reached for his own on a peg on the wall.

After Simon and David went outside, Carmen wiped the counter, poured soap into the dishwasher, closed it, and locked it.

Risa picked up a pink rattle on the table and shook it for her daughter. Francie grabbed at it with a smile.

"I've never seen you look happier," Carmen commented.

"I've never *been* happier," Risa admitted.

"I did have my doubts about Simon, but I can't imagine a better husband or father. Just watching the two of you together—Lucy and Dom, too. I've been wondering…"

When her mother didn't go on, Risa looked up. "What have you been wondering, Mama?"

"I've been wondering if I want to spend the rest of my life alone. I've been wondering if I should go to one of those socials the church has once a month—you know, the one for men and women who are single."

Nothing could have astonished Risa more, or made her happier. "I think you should go for it. Maybe if Lucy and Janetta and I can coordinate our schedules, we can go shopping one evening for something pretty for you to wear." As soon as the words were out of her mouth, Risa wondered if her mother would take offense.

But she didn't. Instead, with a smile and a twinkle in her eye, she confided, "I want to find something Christmassy. Maybe red."

"She wants to buy a red dress?" Simon asked with a grin as he unfastened the buttons of his flannel shirt that night. Risa had just fed Francie and put her to bed.

"That's what she said. You could have knocked me over with a feather."

His shirt hanging open, Simon went to the dresser drawer. Opening it, he took out a small package wrapped in gold foil and decorated with a white bow. He handed it to Risa.

All thoughts of her mother were forgotten. "It's too early for Christmas."

"Sure is. But it's just on time for our second-month anniversary."

Risa was well aware they had been married two months today, but she'd never expected Simon to be aware of the calendar date.

"Open it," he said as she just looked down appreciatively.

Quickly she pulled off the bow and unwrapped the black velvet box. She vividly remembered opening the box that had held her engagement ring the day after the tornado. It had been a marquise-shaped diamond that she glanced at now, seeing how it sparkled from the glow from the bedside lamp. She fingered it and the narrow wedding band often to remind herself how lucky she was.

"You take forever to open presents," Simon teased.

"The anticipation is part of the fun." When she glanced up at him, she saw that he knew exactly what she was talking about.

Unable to wait a moment longer, she lifted open the lid and found a gold heart on a chain. "It's beautiful."

"Let me put it on for you." Simon's voice was husky. After he attached it around her neck, he kissed her nape.

Turning in his arms, she gazed up at him and smiled. "Thank you. I love it. And I love you. My gift for our two-month anniversary is a little less tangible."

Winding his arms around her, he murmured, "I think I'll like that gift best of all."

When Simon kissed her, he filled her world, and Risa knew each anniversary with Simon would only get better. They were lovers, life partners and friends. He was her lawman, and she'd love him till the end of time.

* * * * *

Receive a FREE hardcover book from

HARLEQUIN ROMANCE®

in September!

Harlequin Romance celebrates the launch of the line's new cover design by offering you this exclusive offer valid only in September, only in Harlequin Romance.

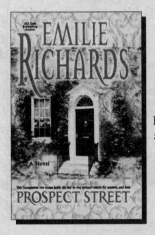

To receive your FREE HARDCOVER BOOK written by bestselling author Emilie Richards, send us four proofs of purchase from any September 2004 Harlequin Romance books. Further details and proofs of purchase can be found in all September 2004 Harlequin Romance books.

Must be postmarked no later than October 31.

Don't forget to be one of the first to pick up a copy of the new-look Harlequin Romance novels in September!

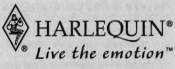

HARLEQUIN®
Live the emotion™

Visit us at www.eHarlequin.com

HRPOP0904

**The *New York Times* bestselling author of
16 Lighthouse Road and *311 Pelican Court*
welcomes you back to Cedar Cove,
where life and love is anything but ordinary!**

DEBBIE MACOMBER

Dear Reader,

I love living in Cedar Cove, but things just haven't been the same
since Max Russell died in our B and B. We still don't have any idea
why he came here and—most important of all—who poisoned him!

But we're not providing the only news in town. I heard that
Maryellen Sherman is getting married and her mother, Grace, has
her pick of interested men—but which one will she choose? And
Olivia Griffin is back from her honeymoon, and her mother, Charlotte,
has a man in her life, too, but I'm not sure Olivia's too pleased....

There's plenty of other gossip I could tell you. Come by for a cup
of tea and one of my blueberry muffins and we'll talk.

44 Cranberry Point

**"Macomber is known for her honest portrayals of
ordinary women in small-town America, and this tale
cements her position as an icon of the genre."**
—***Publishers Weekly*** on *16 Lighthouse Road*

*Available the first week of September 2004,
wherever paperbacks are sold.*

On sale now

girls' night in

21 of today's hottest
female authors
1 fabulous short-story collection
And all for a good cause.

Featuring *New York Times* bestselling authors
Jennifer Weiner (author of *Good in Bed*),
Sophie Kinsella (author of *Confessions of a Shopaholic*),
Meg Cabot (author of *The Princess Diaries*)

Net proceeds to benefit War Child, a network of organizations
dedicated to helping children affected by war.

Also featuring bestselling authors...
Carole Matthews, Sarah Mlynowski, Isabel Wolff, Lynda Curnyn,
Chris Manby, Alisa Valdes-Rodriguez, Jill A. Davis, Megan McCafferty,
Emily Barr, Jessica Adams, Lisa Jewell, Lauren Henderson,
Stella Duffy, Jenny Colgan, Anna Maxted, Adèle Lang,
Marian Keyes and Louise Bagshawe

**RED
DRESS
I N K**
™

www.RedDressInk.com   www.WarChildusa.org
Available wherever trade paperbacks are sold.

™ is a trademark of the publisher.
The War Child logo is the registered trademark of War Child.

RDIGNIMMR

COMING NEXT MONTH

#1738 THEIR LITTLE COWGIRL—Myrna Mackenzie
In a Fairy Tale World...

How can plain-Jane Jackie Hammond be the biological mother of sexy rancher Stephen Collins's adorable daughter when she's never even met him? Ask the fertility clinic! But before Jackie gives up her newfound child, she might discover that her little girl—and the one man who makes Jackie feel beautiful—are worth fighting for.

#1739 GEORGIA GETS HER GROOM!—Carolyn Zane
The Brubaker Brides

Georgia Brubaker has her sights set on the perfect man. But when she comes face-to-face with her childhood nemesis, all her plans go out the window. The nerdy "Cootie Biggles" has developed into supersmooth, 007-clone Carter Biggles-Vanderhousen, who leaves Georgia shaken *and* stirred....

#1740 THE BILLIONAIRE'S WEDDING MASQUER-ADE—Melissa McClone

Billionaires don't make very good farmhands! But Elisabeth Wheeler is desperate for help, and Henry Davenport is strong, available...and handsome. Henry might not have any experience planting or ploughing, but he sure knows how to make Elisabeth's pulse race!

#1741 CINDERELLA'S LUCKY TICKET—
Melissa James

When Lucy Miles tries to claim the house Ben Capriati won in a sweepstakes drawing, he knows he should be furious. But he just can't fight his attraction to the sweet but sassy librarian. Can Ben convince Lucy to build a home with him forever?